the
OPPOSITE

of

YOU

For Juliet, for everything

STRIPES PUBLISHING
An imprint of the Little Tiger Group
1 The Coda Centre, 189 Munster Road, London SW6 6AW

A paperback original
First published in Great Britain in 2017

ISBN: 978-1-84715-727-0

the OPPOSITE of YOU

LOU MORGAN

Stripes

"My sister and I, you will recollect, were twins,
and you know how subtle are the links which bind
two souls which are so closely allied."

Arthur Conan Doyle, *The Adventure of the Speckled Band*

Prologue

Imagine two rooms, side by side in a house. Built to be identical in every way, they have the same windows, looking out on to the same view, the same cupboards, the same doors – even down to the hinges.

But there are differences between them. In one, the bed is against the wall; in the other, it's beside the window. There are different pictures on walls that have been painted different colours. Different cushions, different chairs, different rugs on the floors.

Each room is individual and completely self-contained ... except for the door that connects them.

Once it stood wide open, turning two rooms into one. Once it was always kept unlocked and could swing open and closed as it pleased. But that was a long time ago and things change. Rooms change. People change. Now the only evidence the door still exists is an outline beneath the wallpaper. But even when it's papered over and forgotten, a door is still a door.

And doors are meant to be opened.

1

Bex

She couldn't hear the shouting any more. There was a brief, angry silence – and then feet on the stairs.

Three. Two. One...

Naomi's bedroom door slammed so hard that everything in Bex's room rattled and one of the postcards propped on her shelf fell over and slipped behind the radiator.

"Great. Thanks, Noom."

Bex dropped her revision cards back on her desk, glancing at the clock. Four thirty. Which meant Naomi had lasted through a whole five minutes of conversation with their parents. Sensing the storm that was coming, Bex had excused herself from the kitchen when her twin came home and gone upstairs to try and cram in a few more precious minutes' worth of study.

"Naomi!"

Her dad's voice, from the bottom of the stairs.

Naomi's bedroom door didn't answer. It never did. Naomi was the one who slammed doors and burned bridges.

"Here we go again," Bex said to her room as she picked

her way across the floor, hopping over the revision notes spread over the carpet and stepping out on to the landing. Their father was at the bottom of the stairs, looking up.

His face brightened when he saw her. "Bex – your sister…"

"I'm already going," she said. She raised a hand to knock on Naomi's door, then stopped, her knuckles hovering just above the surface. It was very quiet in there. Normally when Naomi was in one of her moods there would be music blasting out…

"Naomi?" She knocked lightly.

Bex looked back over her shoulder at her dad, who gave her a thumbs-up, then retreated to the kitchen.

"Noom, it's only me. Come on…"

"I don't want to talk about it."

"I heard everything – I didn't mean to, but…" Still nothing. "Please? It's *me*…"

"Jesus, *what?*" The door was flung open and Bex found herself staring at her mirror image – only her mirror image was wearing thick black eyeliner. "Haven't you got revision to do?"

"Haven't you?" Bex shot back automatically, forgetting for a second that she was meant to be calming things down. It was hard sometimes not to let Naomi push her buttons, but she took a deep breath and let it go. There was no sign anywhere of notes or textbooks, despite the fact they both had the same exam the next morning. However, Naomi's laptop was open and she was clearly in the middle of *something*.

Naomi stormed back to her desk and slammed the laptop shut. "It's one final exam. Who cares? Besides, *you're* obviously not fussed, seeing as you're going to Kay's tonight."

"That's revision and you know it." Bex knew this wasn't going to help, so she shrugged and said, "Are you OK?"

"Am I OK?" Naomi repeated the question, but her tone was flat, mocking.

"You can talk to me. I'm on your side, remember?" Bex said gently.

"It's none of your business."

"Fine." Bex wasn't going to let Naomi see how much it stung. And then she spotted the plastic charm bracelet sitting beside Naomi's laptop and any sympathy she felt instantly evaporated.

"Why've you got my lucky bracelet?" Bex snatched it up from the desk. It was stupid, really – a cheap charm bracelet she'd won in the arcade on the pier at Weston-super-Mare. The metal chain left a horrible green line around her wrist, and most of the paint had chipped off the dangling charms, but she'd worn it for every one of her GCSE exams and it had become a talisman.

Naomi didn't answer. She fidgeted with a loose thread

on the hem of her T-shirt. It was a new one: yet another electro band that Bex had never heard of. Then finally she said, "Are you still here?"

"Still waiting for an answer."

"Don't wait too long. Wouldn't want to keep precious Kay waiting, would you? Kay and ... what's-his-face."

"Ralph. You know his name's Ralph, so stop being such a dick about him."

"Whatever. He's ... beige. They both are. Bex and her amazingly beige mates."

"They could have been your friends, too," Bex said quietly.

"Yeah, well. Some of us aren't eleven any more."

Bex pulled the door shut behind her and went downstairs, grabbing her overnight bag from just inside her bedroom door on the way. She could hear their parents talking in the kitchen – her foot hit the creaky step halfway down and the voices stopped abruptly. Then her dad's head appeared around the open kitchen door.

"Oh, it's just you," he said.

"Thanks for making me feel like a vital part of this family, Dad. Love you, too." Bex dropped her overnight bag on the hall floor and went into the kitchen.

"Hello, darling," her mum said. "Are you off to Kay's now?"

"In a minute," Bex said. Her mother was already wearing

her nurse's uniform. "What times does your shift start?"

"Seven." Her mum swallowed a sip of tea.

Her dad carried on talking as if Bex wasn't there. "Naomi's just … acting out. It's very common – especially in twins… She's had enough warnings. Grounding her is our only option."

"You can't ground her! Tomorrow's our last exam – she'll miss the party!"

Her parents exchanged glances. "The last thing your sister needs is another party," her dad said. "It's not up for discussion, Bex. Now, good luck for the morning. I'm sure you'll do fine." And with that, he left the room.

She tried one last time. "Mum – about Naomi…"

"No, Bex. I know you think our grounding her is unfair, but we've just got to get you both through this last exam and then in a few days we'll all be on holiday together. That'll be nice."

Bex pondered her mother's definition of 'nice'. Five hours stuck in the back of the car with Naomi pouting, Dad banging on about his latest marathon training plan and Mum trying to get everyone to 'join in' with the crossword from the front seat…

Her mother's voice pulled Bex back from her thoughts. "…she'll be fine. But if she thinks we're going to let her get away with that kind of behaviour…"

"But Mum…"

"Look, it isn't forever. Now, promise you won't stay up too late tonight?"

"We won't." Based on how she'd been feeling the last few days, it was all she'd be able to do to stay awake past dinner. As soon as the exams were over and the party was done, her plan was to get into her pyjamas and watch Netflix until she was forced to get in the car for the trek to Norfolk.

For Bex, the exams were one more step along the path to the Glasgow School of Art's sculpture course. Pass her exams, do her A levels, go to art school, get her own studio. She had it all planned out. Naomi would probably do what she always did: disappear off to do whatever she happened to be into at that moment. Last summer, it had been wild swimming, the year before, cheerleading. Most recently, it was a creative writing group and hanging out with the guy she'd met there – Simeon. Only one thing about Naomi didn't seem to change. Wherever she went now, whatever she did, Naomi thought it was nobody else's business.

2

Bex

3 months earlier

The brakes of the bus hiss as it pulls away into the traffic, leaving Bex and Naomi on the pavement. Naomi is still tapping away on her phone – she has been the whole way in. Bex dodges a swooping seagull and looks up at the concrete-grey sky.

"So…" she starts, waiting for Naomi to finish her message. Nothing. Her twin doesn't even look up. "I was thinking… St Nick's?"

Naomi rolls her eyes.

"What? You were the one who wanted to come into town." Bex ignores her sister's mumbled answer and tries to summon more enthusiasm than she feels. Their little expedition isn't exactly off to the best start. "Anyway, the Nails market's on – I thought we could go and look through the vintage. They were supposed to be getting more boots in."

"I'd rather catch a skin parasite," Naomi says, dropping her phone into the pocket of her jacket. "Oh no – wait. If I buy a load of manky old clothes, I probably will."

"You can't catch anything from them. Come on, Noom."

"I really, really don't want to spend my Saturday rummaging through – no, watching *you* rummage through racks of grandma clothes, OK?"

"So what did you want to come in for?"

"Not that."

"You're missing the point, you know."

"Of vintage? Enlighten me."

"It's unique."

Naomi twists her mouth. "And this has absolutely nothing to do with the fact Kay's dad took her to that big vintage fair last weekend? So much for being unique."

"Fine. You don't want to come to St Nick's. Where do you want to go?"

Naomi shrugs. "Wherever."

"*Wherever*? Seriously?"

"Why do you care?"

"Why do I...?" Without realizing it, Bex's voice has been getting louder and louder. She takes a deep breath. "OK. So. How about I go to St Nick's, and you go ... wherever and we meet up later?"

"Fine."

"Half twelve at the benches in Cabot Circus?"

"The ones you always insist we meet at? Oh my God, Rebecca Harper couldn't *possibly* do something *original*, could she?"

Bex frowns. "I'll see you later."

Naomi stomps off – and then, on the other side of the street, Bex spots a familiar face.

"Kay! KAY! Hey! Wait up…"

⌇◦⌇

Kay tries on everything. From boots to hats to belts, scarves, a waistcoat with glittery red stripes that neither of them would be seen dead in, to a skirt that looks like something Kay's great-aunt would wear. Finally Kay buys a floppy hat and Bex picks out a tiny beaded bag.

"Ooooh. For prom?" Kay asks, peering over her shoulder as she pays.

"Dunno." Bex takes her change and the paper carrier bag. "I haven't even thought about prom yet. It's months off, and there's the exams and the class party and…"

"What a lie!" Kay snorts. "You've *so* thought about it. You're wondering whether Orson'll actually ask you, aren't you?"

"No!" Bex feels her cheeks burning. "I'm not, actually."

"Mmmmhmmm?"

"Can we just drop… Oh no." Bex stops dead in her tracks, staring at a clock on a nearby stall.

"What? What's the matter?"

"Naomi! I was supposed to meet her!" She scrambles for her phone.

"When?"

"Nearly an hour ago."

"Oh, whoops!" Kay says. "Just tell her you got held up."

"I've got no reception! Can I use yours?"

Kay sighs and pulls out her phone. "No signal, either. Where were you going to meet her?"

Bex groans and taps out a message to Naomi, hitting send in hope.

"Cabot Circus," she sighs.

Bex leaves Kay at the door to Topshop, dodging through the crowds of Saturday shoppers to the benches where she agreed to meet Naomi, a guilty ache in the pit of her stomach.

The benches are busy: a group of girls from the year below at school, a couple of families with toddlers and an old man with a stained parka…

But no Naomi.

Bex sits on the edge of the nearest bench: the only spot is next to Old Man Parka and she quickly realizes why. She pulls her phone out – full reception. And not a single message, even though hers to Naomi has gone: it must have sent as soon as she picked up a signal.

She tries Naomi's phone. It rings and rings and finally goes to voicemail. Sighing, she hangs up and dials another number. There's no point leaving a message – she knows Naomi never checks them.

"Kay? Yeah. No, she's probably gone home. You still in Topshop? No – wait there. I'll come to you."

3

Naomi

Naomi stormed out of the kitchen, her dad's words still burning in her ears, banging her bag into the banister as she went. She hadn't meant to be out so late last night – and, to be fair, she really had forgotten there was an exam that morning. She'd thought it was a revision day and who cared about them, anyway? Besides, how was she to know that her dad would wait up for her until 4 a.m.? The less said about how she'd felt by that point, the better, even if she'd thought she covered it pretty well… And hadn't she gone in and sat the exam anyway?

Bex was already home by the time Naomi got in from school, pouring herself a glass of juice from the fridge. She spotted her sister's gaze flick to their parents, who were talking quietly on the other side of the room. Her dad's face tensed, and Bex downed her drink and slipped away.

Then the lecture began. They were concerned she wasn't happy, concerned she wasn't being honest with them, concerned about her choices…

And what was their solution? To ground her.

"And that's it? You're just going to send me to my room like some ... *kid*?"

"If you're going to behave like a child, Naomi, then we have no choice but to treat you like one."

"You never treat me like anything else!" she snapped. "Not like Bex. Bex gets to…"

"Your sister has shown us she's responsible. She has *earned* our trust."

"I said I was sorry! I made a mistake, fine. All I'm asking for is a chance – *one* chance. But no. Fine. Whatever. Thanks a *lot*." Naomi stormed out and ran up the stairs. When she reached her room, she slammed the door so hard she felt the whole house rattle.

Whenever there was a problem, she could always sense the question in the air: *why can't you be more like your sister?*

"Because I'm not her," Naomi said to her empty room, throwing her bag into the corner and pulling out her laptop.

She dropped into her desk chair and let out a deep sigh.

"Not your finest moment, Naomi," she mumbled to the screen. But the way the mood had shifted when she walked into the kitchen ... it had made her feel like an outsider in her own family.

No, you're overthinking it, she told herself, checking her messages. *It's just been a bad day.*

On the other side of the door, Naomi could feel her sister. Waiting.

"Naomi?"

There was a quiet knock.

Naomi stopped her chair spinning and stared at the door.

"Naomi?"

Naomi rubbed her eyes, then wiped at the edges of the lids with the cuff of her sleeve, scrubbing away a smudge of eyeliner. She wasn't going to let her sister see her cry.

Naomi tiptoed across her bedroom to the door but she didn't open it. *I don't want to do this. I don't want you to come and check up on me.*

"Noom, it's only me. Come on…"

"I don't want to talk about it."

"Please. It's *me*…"

Naomi pulled open the door and there on the landing, looking straight back at her, was Bex.

4

Bex

"Here we go. It's on. Day of." Kay was sounding way too perky.

"Day of what, exactly?" Bex asked.

"Day of the last exam. Day of judgement, day of *days*!"

"You are far too excited about this exam. Why *are* you so excited, anyway?" Bex smothered a yawn.

"The real question is why you *aren't*? This is the *last one*. And besides, it's what comes after that matters."

"The party?"

"The party."

"You know it's *just* a party, right? And it's only at Dominic's house – he's going to be as much of a prat as he always is. Like last year, when..."

"But – but, but, but – I heard that Dominic's parents have said he can use the swimming pool this time." Kay waved Bex's comments aside.

"You hate swimming."

"I hate swimming at the *leisure centre*. This is Dominic's pool. His actual pool in his actual garden. And ...

Dominic's older brother is home from boarding school."
Kay let the sentence hang in the air.

"Mike?"

"He prefers *Michael* now. And he's baaaa-aack!" Kay
sang the last word, her eyes sparkling.

"Ralph will kill you. He's had a thing for Mike…"

"Michael."

"Whatever – for the last three years. You can't go after
the object of his adoration."

"Too bad for Ralph."

"Who, might I remind you, is one of your best friends."

"Yeah? So are you, and I'd push *you* out of a plane if
you were standing in between me and Michael Anderson.
Anyway, are you wearing your shitty bracelet?"

Bex held up her wrist and rattled the charms.

"Right then. What's there to worry about?" Kay beamed.

Bex gave up.

Kay stopped to check her hair in the window of the
antique mirror shop in the middle of town. Bex usually
tried to avoid looking – it was creepy seeing her reflection
multiplied over and over and over. She always half
expected one of her images to move, because how could
there be that many and none of them be Naomi?

If Kay's phone hadn't beeped, she could easily have

spent another fifteen minutes fiddling with her hair. She squinted at the screen in the bright morning light. "Ralph's already at school. He says he'll see us outside the exam room."

"Of course he's already there." Bex laughed. "He's probably been there since the end of the last exam." She slid her arm through her best friend's. "Come on. Your hair's not getting any better," she said with a grin.

"Hey!"

"I mean … how could it? You know, it being perfect already."

"More like it. In a couple of hours, we'll be finished and Michael will be irresistibly drawn to my…"

"A couple of hours?" Bex looked at her watch. "Wow. You must work fast – we'll barely even have got out of school by then."

"This is my happy place, Bex. Stop trying to harsh it." Kay clasped her hands together like she was praying. "And please, please, please, no resits. No. Resits."

"Like you've ever needed to resit anything." Still arm in arm, they stepped off the pavement and on to the road. A memory of her and Naomi after their Year Six exams popped into Bex's head.

"How do you think you did?"

"Same as you."

"I didn't tell you how I did."

25

"I know. But I did the same. You'll see."

"Watch out…!" Bex was hauled back from her thoughts as Kay yanked her across the road out of the way of a black Transit van. The driver must only have seen them at the last second, because there was a squeal of brakes as both girls tumbled on to the pavement. Kay was on her feet again in a second, swearing furiously and making obscene gestures at the van as it disappeared down the road. When she'd finished yelling, she turned back to Bex, her eyes widening. "Your elbow! You're bleeding!"

"Do you think it's enough to be excused?" Bex examined her arm. "If we tell them we almost died, maybe they'll let us off the exam?"

"So, you're OK?" Kay frowned. "Hey, there's Vikram!" She waved, nearly smacking Bex in the face. "Oops. Sorry."

Bex smiled at her friend, but there was a chilly sensation in the pit of her stomach, somewhere between excitement and fear. Maybe it was the shock of the near-miss. Maybe it was adrenaline, or even plain old pre-exam nerves. It would all be over in a few hours anyway.

The stairs up to the exam room were still almost empty and their footsteps echoed on the bare concrete. Other than Kay's footsteps, all Bex could really hear was

Mrs Blewitt's voice from the cloakroom droning on about not leaving phones switched on in their bags. "At least we won't have to listen to that twice a day any more," she muttered under her breath.

Ralph was sitting on the top step, right in front of the closed door.

"Early enough for you?" she said to Ralph with a smile.

"You can never be too early," Ralph said, shaking his head. He obviously wasn't in the mood for jokes – he didn't even really look up when she said it.

If she was honest, Bex wasn't really in the mood for joking, either – something felt wrong, as though there was sand under her skin and no amount of scratching could get it out. A queue of students was beginning to form down the stairway, but Naomi wasn't among them. Bex peered over the handrail, through the square spiral of the stairs to the ground floor, hoping to catch a glimpse of her sister, but there was no sign.

Bex drummed her fingers on the stair rail.

"Hey. You OK?" Kay's voice seemed to come from a very long way off.

"What? Oh. Oh, yeah. Just looking for Naomi. I can't see her." Bex turned back to her friends.

"You're her sister, not her mother. Stop acting like you're responsible for her."

"I'm sure she's around," Ralph said. "There's probably

just a big queue for the toilets. Which is what happens if you don't get here *early*..." He poked Kay and she stuck her tongue out at him.

Bex tuned them both out and looked at her watch again. "Do you think...?" she started – but she didn't get to finish, because there was the sound of footsteps, then a handle turning, and the door behind Ralph swung open.

Their exam desks were assigned alphabetically by surname, so technically Bex and Naomi were seated one after the other but the layout meant Bex's desk was at the front, while Naomi's was at the very back in the next row. As she shuffled to her seat, something at the back of Bex's mind kept niggling at her; something between a memory and a thought, and which slipped up from a crack between the two.

Their first day at school, walking in hand in hand. Two teachers waiting for them in the office and the horror of understanding that they weren't going to be allowed to stay together.

"Follow me," said one, speaking only to Bex, not to Naomi. It was unthinkable. But she followed and she heard her twin's voice calling her name all the way along the corridor and round the corner ... and she could still hear it in her head even after the teacher had led her to her new form room.

Bex had never forgotten it. But why was she thinking of it now? The memory felt like a scar. She tried to put

Naomi out of her mind and focus, running the tip of her finger over the long gouge in the wood that someone had made, probably waiting for another exam to start. She laid out her things and checked her watch for the fiftieth time. She was ready.

"Turn your papers over … now."

Bex was halfway through writing her student number on the front of her answer booklet when she realized what was wrong with that memory of their first day.

She hadn't been led away first.

It wasn't her memory.

It was Naomi's.

⌇

"Pens down, please. Your time is up. Yes, Matthew, that means you, too."

There was a collective sigh as everyone stretched, shuffled papers or put their heads down on their desks in relief. That was it.

"Congratulations, Year Eleven. You've finished. Please remain in your seats until your answer booklets have been collected."

Bex gulped down the last mouthful of water from her bottle as the teachers bustled about the room collecting papers. The deputy head strode past her desk with a waft of aftershave and bounded up on to the podium at the

29

front of the room. He whispered something to the lead invigilator, who shook her head. Bex felt her face turning a hot red as both members of staff swivelled to look right at her.

Had she done something wrong?

Bex thought back over the exam, over the queue on the stairs, back to stashing her bag in the cloakroom…

Nope. It was the same as always.

So why were they still staring at her?

Bex sat glued to her seat with her exam paper in front of her, waiting.

After what felt like a week, a voice came from just behind her shoulder. "Answer book, please."

Everything was *fine*, she told herself. In a minute she'd be collecting her bag and heading out into the sunshine with Ralph and Kay, and she'd find Naomi and everything would be OK.

And then…

"Rebecca? Your parents have rung the office and left a message."

"A message?" Bex heard her voice as though it belonged to someone else.

"Can you head home straight away, please? They said it's important."

"What about Naomi? Does she…" Bex turned in her seat, looking towards the back of the room. The desks around her had emptied, but they were still collecting papers further back. At the far end of her row, she saw Dexter hand his in and slide out of his desk, heading for the door – and behind him, Sarah, in tears.

When Sarah stood, Bex could see that Naomi's seat was empty, the exam paper untouched in the middle of her desk.

Naomi hadn't turned up to the exam. At all.

Maybe she'd got ill or fallen down the stairs and broken her leg. But why was it so urgent that Bex went back?

Because she isn't at home.

5

Naomi

3 months earlier

The bus makes a horrible noise as it edges back out into the traffic and Naomi sees Bex wince. Dan keeps sending her messages about a gig and Naomi pokes at her phone to silence it, tapping out a terse reply.

"So…" says Bex. "I was thinking… St Nick's?"

Naomi rolls her eyes.

"What? You were the one who wanted to come into town. Anyway, the Nails market's on – I thought we could go and look through the vintage."

"I'd rather catch a skin parasite," Naomi says, silently adding 'than copy anything Kay does'. Bex narrows her eyes at her… Can her sister tell what she's thinking?

Of course not. She hasn't for years.

They bicker like they always do these days – especially when Kay's involved. However much she tries, Naomi can't help it. She hasn't ever told Bex about that awful conversation back at the start of secondary school and she never will. It would only sound petty and stupid. Sometimes she wonders whether Kay ever realized she was talking to the wrong twin. Sometimes, Naomi wonders whether that conversation had always been meant for her...

"Half twelve at the benches in Cabot Circus?"

She leaves her sister on the pavement and walks away, not really thinking about where until she feels her phone buzz. Pulling it out of her bag, her heart sinks when she sees it's Dan again – still banging on about that gig. With a sigh, she stuffs her phone into her jacket ... and is about to turn round when something catches her eye. A new shop, half hidden down a side street. Its windows are full of wigs on wooden stands...

The bell over the door chimes as she steps back out on to the street, swinging a plastic bag with 'Wonderland Wigs' swirled across it in neon script. She feels better about earlier – if she'd had Bex with her, she wouldn't have been able to go into the shop. How could she have explained the wig to her sister? But she's pleased with her find – it's an electric-blue bob, and somehow it makes her look older and ... different.

With a spring in her step, she heads back to Cabot Circus to meet her sister, stopping to pick up a magazine on the way and throwing away the Wonderland Wigs carrier. She slides the packed-up wig into the newsagent's bag. Bex will never know.

Naomi flips through the pages of the magazine. She checks her phone. Bex is ten minutes late.

She waits. She checks her phone again: no messages. No missed calls.

She tries to call Bex but the call goes straight to voicemail. She thinks about leaving a message, but wouldn't it sound pathetic? 'Where are you? I'm waiting for you...' No. She puts the phone away.

Around her, people are coming and going. Walking arm in arm or hand in hand, talking and laughing. None of them are alone. Not like Naomi, sitting and waiting for her sister – who is now over half an hour late. No message. Nothing.

Naomi scuffs the toe of her shoe against the foot of the bench, and catches herself trying to talk to Bex in her head.

Where are you? Aren't you coming?

She stops herself with an angry laugh – she should know better. Maybe they used to be able to talk to one another without speaking and maybe they used to be able to finish each other's sentences, knowing what the other wanted to say or needed to hear ... but not any more.

Forty-five minutes.

And the longer she sits and waits ... the more she wonders whether she actually hates her sister.

When Bex is an hour late Naomi's eyes start to burn, prickling with hot tears she isn't about to let anyone see. She jumps up, snatching her bag from the bench, and hurries through the wide doorway of the public toilets. Splashing water on her face, she pulls herself together and stares at her reflection.

"I should give it up, shouldn't I? Me and Bex, we're just … not. Not any more," she says to the mirror.

"What was that? Give what up, love?" asks a little old lady in a navy raincoat at the sink beside hers.

Naomi doesn't answer. Instead she smooths down her hair, picks up her carrier bag and walks back out towards the bench…

Only to spot Bex standing right in front of the space she's just left, frantically looking around.

Before she can think about why she's doing it, Naomi ducks back behind a pillar.

A man walking past does a double-take. "Did you see that?" he asks his friend. "Identical twins, mate!"

Naomi doesn't want to be half of a matching pair. What's the point of it, anyway? No, she wants to be *Naomi* – not one of the two Harper twins. Identical in every way except…

Except that Bex is happy. Bex knows who she's supposed to be.

Naomi risks a peek around the pillar.

Bex is still there, sitting down next to the old man with the grotty coat.

Naomi looks at the bag in her hand.

She goes back into the toilets ... and a couple of minutes later, wearing her new blue wig, she walks straight past her sister.

Bex doesn't see her: of course she doesn't – because she isn't really looking for *Naomi*. She's looking for her own mirror image.

6

Naomi

"So, are you coming – or what?"

Dan sounded impatient and, at the other end of the phone, Naomi could hear him fiddling with something – probably rolling a cigarette. He thought smoking made him more interesting. It didn't. She'd told him that when she met him: it was pretty much the first thing she had ever said to him at that Freshers' fair over at the university. She'd snuck in, hoping nobody would question her or ask what she was doing there: she'd even had a cover story ready about looking for her older sister. It wasn't like she'd meant to stay – she just wanted to see what was going on – but then people started talking to her like she belonged there. Like she was one of *them*. Who was she to tell them they were wrong?

Naomi chewed on her lip, trying to decide whether she even wanted to go to the party he was talking about. On the one hand, there was the fact she'd been grounded and the small matter of that last exam: tomorrow's maths paper. But if she didn't know the work by now, what good was staring at it all night going to do? What she needed was a break. A chance to relax, refocus.

Before their first exam, Dad had collared them on the way out of the door and given both Naomi and Bex the 'it's important to relax' pep talk ... so *technically*, if she went to the party, it might be *good* for her studies.

Naomi laughed, trying to keep quiet. With her father already in bed, Bex over at Kay's and Mum working the overnight shift at the hospital, the house was silent.

"What's so funny?"

"Nothing. Send me the address and I'll see you there."

Dan hung up but Naomi kept hold of the phone and before she realized what she was doing, she'd scrolled through her contacts to Simeon's name. A tiny thumbnail photo of his face smiled out at her. She threw her phone at her bed so hard it bounced off and landed on the floor.

"Shallow," he'd called her.

It had hurt.

Naomi had thought they were good together. Anyway, she thought, he took himself and the overwritten crap he brought to their creative writing group far too seriously. And then there'd been that final dig – that she wasn't 'spontaneous'.

"Not spontaneous. Like he knows anything about me," she muttered to her room.

It wasn't like anyone would miss her for an hour or two...

She slipped on her favourite denim jacket, rummaging

in the drawer of her desk with one hand until her fingers closed on the envelope of cash she kept stashed away and pulled out a couple of notes. She jammed them into the pocket of the jacket and scooped her phone up off the floor then, without a second thought, she swung open her window and climbed out on to the sill before sliding lightly down the old metal drainpipe … just like she had a dozen times before.

Grounded.

Sure.

⌘

Once they got into the party, they stuck to the rules. Keep moving, never talk to the same person for too long. Naomi had it down to a fine art. All it took to belong somewhere was to pretend you already did.

Across the room, Dan was nodding and looking serious as he made a show of listening to some guy in a lumberjack shirt with a man-bun. A couple of drinks later, she saw him deep in conversation with a girl with flowers and vines tattooed down her arms.

Naomi accepted a shot of peppermint vodka from a tall blond guy, tipping her head back to throw it straight down her throat. Simeon's smirk flashed through her mind, and the vodka felt hot and cold all the way down.

Was it bothering her so much because she'd thought

they were better together than he did? Or was it the nagging worry that he'd seen who she *really* was and it hadn't been good enough?

She wouldn't make that mistake again in a hurry.

She grabbed another glass, and then, behind her: "Hey! Hi there! It's Naomi, right?" A voice she recognized. Someone who recognized her, too – but which Naomi? The quiet one who wrote clever stories? The sporty girl from last summer? Or music-mad Naomi who was supposedly in her first year at uni and working for the student radio station: the wild, smart-mouthed version of herself?

With a smile, she turned. The guy who had spoken was a little taller than her, slim, with dark hair artfully messed. "It's me. Ethan! We met at that gig a few weeks back… At the Louisiana?" His eyes moved over her face, but they didn't seem to be entirely focused.

"Ethan! Ohmygodhiiiiiii!" She fixed a wide-eyed and beaming smile on her face. "What are you doing here?"

"Celebrating." He waved his beer and white froth sloshed out. "We've got another gig. A pretty big one, actually. At a festival."

"You have? That's amazing! When is it?"

"Tomorrow." He beamed at her. "We were the alternates for a slot, and we just got the call yesterday that the lead singer for the other band broke his arm.

Which is amazing."

Not for that guy, it isn't, she thought. "Oh, wow! Where? I'll see if I can make it…"

"It's at Hemisphere." He puffed out his chest as he said it and Naomi realized why he'd been so pleased to see her. He wanted to show off.

"Oh. My. God. That's huge! Congratulations!"

"It's not on one of the big stages or anything, but it's still a massive deal – and there'll be loads of industry people there." He took a swig of his beer and grinned at her. "So … maybe we'll get lucky, right?"

"Are you kidding? You guys are basically my favourite band already. I'd come to see you!" Was she laying it on too thick, she wondered? Looking at Ethan's broad smile, she doubted it.

Out of the corner of her eye she saw Dan tap his watch pointedly. He was telling her to move on. Any second now, that 'Where-Do-You-Know-So-And-So-From…?' question would pop up and then the game would be up…

"…ask you something?"

"Sorry – what?"

"Why don't you come with us?"

"What?"

"To Hemisphere. Why not? We've got a spare pass." Ethan leaned closer to her and she could feel the clammy heat of him, smell his sweat… She fought the urge to

41

step back. "It was meant to be my girlfriend's but she can't get out of work."

"That's too bad. She must be disappointed."

"I dunno. I'm not even sure she actually tried to get the time off, you know? She's just not…"

"Spontaneous?" The word slipped out of her mouth before she could stop it.

His eyes lit up. "Exactly. Spontaneous. And then I saw you here, like it was meant to be or something. And maybe you can get some stuff for the radio station – an interview, or…?"

"That would be the best."

"Awesome. So it's a date. Well. Not a 'date'. You know. Because … girlfriend, yeah?"

Did he just wink at her? Naomi's skin crawled. "I'll tell the others – you can ride with us in the van. We're heading there straight after this, so stick around."

"Wait – tonight?"

"Yeah. Our slot's tomorrow afternoon."

"Tomorrow." She couldn't go. She couldn't possibly go. Her exam…

Not. Spontaneous. Enough.

She lifted the empty shot glass and waggled it. "I'd love to come with you."

It was more than one drink later when Naomi stepped out into the garden, taking a second to steady herself, then shutting the patio door behind her. The party was slowly dying down. Above her, the sky had brightened through shades of orange and salmon into purpled-blue, and she could hear birds chirping in a tree nearby. The house – whoever's it was – backed on to the woods and everything outside was peaceful. Naomi closed her eyes and tipped her head back.

Inside, Ethan had stumbled off in search of the other members of his band – specifically, he said, Ollie: their drummer and the actual owner (and driver) of the van, who had been trying to get some sleep upstairs. More than once she'd found herself wanting to tell him she couldn't go; she couldn't just … run off.

An image of her parents flickered through her mind. An image of Bex. What would they think when they realized she was gone? Would they even have noticed that she hadn't been safely tucked up in her room all night?

She couldn't just go… Could she?

Naomi opened her eyes and looked. High above her a bird wheeled against the fast-lightening sky. Nothing tied it down. Nothing held it back. It was alone up there with miles of space around it…

No matter how far away she went or who she pretended to be, somewhere her twin would still be there. A thought, a suggestion, a *feeling*. Bex might have forgotten how things used to be, but Naomi hadn't. She could still feel it, the thing that linked them like an unbroken umbilical cord. A thread that tied them together.

Which was worse, she wondered – to be lonely and alone or to never be alone and be lonely anyway?

Around her more birds joined the dawn chorus as the world woke up. It felt like she was on the edge of something, on the threshold of something new. All she had to do was take the next step.

Behind her, she heard someone clearing their throat.

Ethan.

"You ready? We're going to head off in a minute if you still want to come?"

"Yes! I am definitely, definitely ready."

"D'you want us to swing by your place to get your stuff?"

She hadn't even thought about what she might need – in her head, she'd pictured herself climbing into the back of their van, slamming the door and just … going.

"That would be great. I'll run in and get a change of clothes. I don't need much." She'd get them to park round the corner, shin up the drainpipe and grab her stuff – and then she'd be away. In and out and no one would know.

"You really are spontaneous. I like it!"

They tiptoed back through the house. There were

people asleep on sofas. Beer and whisky bottles littered the floor, along with a scattering of empty glasses.

Naomi's toe caught the side of a half-empty vodka bottle and before she could grab it, it tipped over. "Whoops."

Nobody seemed to be awake enough to notice, and Ethan led her through the front door and out to a battered black Transit van. Huddled around it were the rest of the band. The guy leaning against the driver's door was sipping black coffee from a paper cup. He eyed her carefully.

"You must be Naomi. I'm Ollie. Drummer – and today, the designated driver. Where's your stuff?"

"We're stopping off at hers on the way. It's cool," Ethan spoke for her.

Ollie raised a suspicious eyebrow and she shrugged.

"I travel pretty light. I'll give you directions."

"We really need to hit the road. It's a fair few hours' drive and that's if the traffic isn't already grim."

"I'll literally be in and out, I promise."

For a moment it looked like he was going to say something but Ethan came to the rescue, slinging his arm round Ollie's neck and accidentally knocking the coffee out of his hand in the process.

"Watch it, Eeth. Jesus, you're wrecked. Try and get some sleep, will you? You're no good to us in this state."

"Yeah, yeah." Ethan shrugged. "We're good. Let's roll!"

He banged on the side of the van and the others groaned. One by one they clambered in; Naomi following them as Ollie brushed the drops of coffee off his jeans. The van wasn't exactly huge and between the three other band members piling into the seats (none of whom bothered to say hello, but immediately settled down to sleep) and the band's kit, it was a squeeze in the back. Ethan rolled his jacket into a ball and tucked it under his head. He was snoring loudly by the time they reached the end of the road.

In the front seat, Ollie rested his elbow on the bass drum that was strapped into the front passenger spot and craned his neck to speak to her. "Where's your place?"

"Head towards the big roundabout, and it's a couple of streets from there. I'll tell you where you need to turn."

～◯～

Ollie didn't seem particularly bothered that she pulled herself over the fence at the side of the house instead of walking in through the front door.

She grabbed the open window and gave it a gentle tug. It swung out far enough for her to scramble in. Pulling herself to her feet, she stopped, holding her breath and listening for any sign of life.

Nothing.

Her mum wouldn't be back from her shift for a good

half hour, so all she had to worry about was her dad coming back from his run before she could grab her stuff. But if he was out this early in the morning, it was likely to be a ten-miler, and she wasn't going to hang around.

Hurrying around her room, she picked up her school bag ... then thought better of it. In the bottom of her cupboard she found the old rucksack she'd used for her cheerleading kit. Bundling up some clothes, her blue wig, an old plastic poncho and a blanket, she stuffed them into the bag – then pulled the envelope of cash out of her drawer and shoved that into the zipped pocket at the back.

"Tent. Shit."

Naomi bit her lip. She didn't think the enormous one in the shed would be any good.

She'd figure something out.

All that was left was for her to grab her wellies from the bottom of her wardrobe and...

Halfway across the room, a stab of guilt stopped her in her tracks. She shuffled through the junk that littered her desk for a notebook.

Needed some time. I'm sorry. I'm fine. With friends. Will be back soon. Don't worry. N x

It should, at least, stop them thinking she'd been abducted, but was vague enough that she didn't need to worry about her father turning up and hauling her home.

She scooped her laptop off the desk and slid it into its usual hiding place under her bed, then she turned off her phone and pocketed it.

Leaning out of the window, she dropped her wellington boots down on to the lawn, then slung her bag on to her shoulder. Halfway down the drainpipe, it did dawn on her that she could have simply walked down the stairs, but by that point it was a little late.

As Ollie started the van engine, she wedged herself back into her seat. The others didn't show any sign of stirring. She leaned her head against the side of the van and dozed.

By the time the van braked to avoid hitting her twin sister, Naomi was fast asleep and dreaming.

7

Bex

Bex closed the front door behind her. The house was unnervingly quiet.

"Naomi? Is that…?"

Their mother appeared in the kitchen doorway.

"It's just me, Mum," Bex said. "What's going on? Where's Naomi?"

"Naomi isn't here," said her dad, coming to stand just behind her mum. "She's gone."

"Gone? Gone where?"

Her dad held out a piece of paper: a note, scrawled in Naomi's untidy handwriting. "We were hoping you could tell us."

"*Me?*"

"You aren't in trouble. We just want to know where she is."

"I don't know."

"You expect us to believe that?"

"It's the truth!" Bex stared at her parents, open-mouthed. Her fingers had closed around the note and turned it into nothing more than a crumpled ball of paper.

Where's Naomi? Where's Naomi? Where's Naomi?

The thought whirled through her head, round and round and round.

I'm fine. With friends, the note had said.

What friends did Naomi have that she would simply take off with?

There was that Simeon guy ... but from what little she knew, he didn't seem like the type to agree to something so crazy. So who else could it be?

"You're sure there's nothing you want to tell us? You haven't spoken to her...?" Their mother sounded more pleading than their father.

"I don't know anything, I promise. I was at Kay's, we went to school, did the exam ... and that's it."

"She wasn't here when I came back from my run," her dad said, shaking his head. "I thought she'd left early. And then when the school office called, I..."

He bit his lip.

"What in God's name is she *thinking*?" her mum said.

"She'll be fine. I'm sure she will, and this is just..."

"Don't you dare tell me this is her testing her boundaries, Neil."

He pinched the bridge of his nose again. "She's pushing against..."

"No. She's gone too far this time. This is her *future*."

50

"Did you call her?" It felt like a stupid question even as Bex said it, but what else was there to say?

"She isn't answering," her dad said. "Not that that means anything."

With friends.

But who were they? She never had anyone over to the house. And Bex never really pictured Naomi as having friends in the same way Kay and Ralph were hers. Naomi had *people*. People she ate lunch with, and people she sat next to in class. She had people whose homework she copied, and people she would hang out with at break ... but *friends*?

Why did you need time? Where did you go? Who are you with? What the hell are you doing?

While her parents huddled around the phone, Bex grabbed her school bag and fled upstairs – where, in the safety of her room, she flung it against the wall. Her things spilled out on to the floor: pens, revision notes, the T-shirt she'd been wearing the day before that had somehow ended up in there in a muddle – a Christmas present from Naomi last year, printed with an image of a sculpture by Patricia Volk. The sculpture was one of Bex's favourites and she had had no idea how Naomi knew. Her sister had shrugged.

51

"You have a picture of it pinned up in your room."

"I have loads of pictures pinned up in my room. How'd you know it was that one?"

"I just did. Obviously."

She had worn the shirt so much that the fabric was already thin and soft, and the bright turquoise of the sculpted head in the print had turned a summer blue.

Naomi had known that she would love it. Naomi knew her. And she had thought she knew Naomi, for all their differences.

Bex blinked away the hot prickling sensation behind her eyes. She sat on the edge of her bed and stared at the wall above her pillow. There was the Frank Turner photo that Kay and Ralph had given her for her last birthday, a collage of scraps of antique lace and postcards she'd bought on the school trip to the Arnolfini gallery … and in the middle of the jumble, right at the heart of it, a photo of the two of them. Bex and Naomi, aged five or six, playing in the garden. Dressed in their summer clothes, with their hair pulled back into identical ponytails, before Naomi had decided that she wanted short hair. They were standing toe to toe and staring into each other's faces.

"Where did you go?" she asked the empty room. "What are you thinking?"

52

A little while later, there was a knock at the front door, and her heart leaped ... only for her to remember that Naomi would never *knock*.

The police.

There was a heart-stopping second's panic before Bex remembered they were here because they'd been called.

Trying to calm her pounding heart, Bex leaned against her wardrobe, pressing her hands to her head. She had always been the one who hid in there when they played hide-and-seek as kids, slipping back through the hanging clothes as far as she could and trying to lose herself in the dark. And maybe that's why Naomi always found her so quickly – but even on the rare occasions when she'd tried hiding somewhere else, Naomi *always* found her.

"I'll always be able to find you."

"How do you always know?"

"Because we're twins, stupid."

"So?"

"So ... I just do, OK?"

From somewhere in the mess she'd dropped on her floor, her phone bleeped.

Bex rummaged through her things until her fingers closed around her mobile.

It had to be Naomi. It had to be...

She jabbed at the notification icon and held her breath as the message opened.

Hey, where are you? You disappeared! Waited by front gate for ages? Walking into town if you want to catch up! K

It was Kay. Just Kay.

Bex stayed where she was, her phone still in her hand. She didn't know how long she was there, not quite able to move or to think. She should be celebrating right now – *they* should. She'd never felt less like celebrating in her life.

Her fingers moved automatically to Naomi's contact. Her hair was shorter and Bex was less likely to be sticking her tongue out at the camera, but otherwise it was a perfect match.

Dialling NAOMI...

"You have reached the voicemail..."

"It's me. Where *are* you? Call me and let me know you're OK. Mum and Dad have got the police here and everything. Call me. Please."

She hung up and scrolled through her contacts to another number.

Dialling KAY...

"Finally! Where are you? We waited for you for, like, ever." She mumbled something away from the phone. "Ralph wants to know what you want to do about food. I was thinking we'd get a cheeky Nandos before we go over to Dominic's, but he wants KFC because he's classy... Shut up, Ralph. Yes, Nandos *is* still a thing. Anyway, there's a load of people..." Kay stopped suddenly. "Why aren't you talking?"

"It's Naomi."

"Yeah, sure. Pull the other one – you're definitely Bex." Bex could hear Kay laughing.

"She's disappeared. Nobody knows where she is."

Kay's laughter died away. "What?"

"She didn't turn up for the exam. I didn't know until the end. How could I not *know*, Kay? But she didn't come and she's not at home. She's just ... gone." Bex stopped herself from saying more. It would only lead to questions she didn't have the answers to. Like there weren't enough of those already.

"You're kidding...?"

"I'm not."

"The selfish cow!"

"*What?*"

"Oh, come on," Kay snapped. "Don't tell me you're actually falling for this? It's just like that time you won the school art prize..."

"It's nothing like that and you know it."

"Yes, it is. It's another one of her little dramas!"

"It's not. This is different. This is..."

"If the next words out of your mouth even remotely resemble 'not like Naomi', I swear I'm never speaking to you again. This is exactly like her." There was a rustling

55

sound on the line. "Ralph asked me to ask if you're OK. Like I haven't already."

You haven't, thought Bex. "I'm fine, sort of. The police are here."

"Do *you* know where she is?" Kay asked quietly.

"You think I wouldn't have said something if I did?"

"Don't be like that. It's just ... you two are funny sometimes, you know?"

"I don't know *anything* about this!" The words came out louder and angrier than she'd meant them to. "Sorry," said Bex, into the chilly silence. "I think I'll be giving the party a miss."

"I got that."

"Can you maybe ask around at Dominic's – see if anyone's seen her or knows anything?"

"Fine. And when she turns up – which she will, once she's got everybody's attention – I can do the 'I Told You So' dance. Deal?"

"Deal."

Bex sighed and dropped her phone on her desk. Everyone thought they knew who Naomi was and what she would and wouldn't do ... but they didn't. Not really. Naomi never let them.

Bex had always believed, as they grew up and grew apart, that it was a good thing: you were supposed to be at least a little bit different from your twin, weren't you?

Their mum had said it was 'healthy'; that it was good they no longer finished all each other's sentences.

Or maybe it had just been Bex no longer finishing Naomi's sentences...

Bex walked out of her room and across the landing. It felt wrong to go into her sister's room without her; to go through her things ... but she had to know who Naomi *was*. The real Naomi.

Without Naomi in it, the room felt strange. The window was ajar, but the bed was neatly made: wherever she'd gone last night, she hadn't been back.

Bex closed her eyes and stood in the middle of the room.

What am I looking for?

Something that tells me what she was thinking.

Something Mum and Dad would miss; something they wouldn't understand.

Bex knew she was hoping for a sign, a clue – something that would prove to her that she still knew her twin better than anyone else.

I should have known.

Had their parents already looked through Naomi's things? It was hard to tell, her room was such a bombsite. The detritus of Naomi's various 'hobbies' littered the surfaces: bits of an old wetsuit that she'd tried to cut up and turn into a top when she gave up the wild swimming, a baton from her summer of cheerleading, half a broken skateboard. Four different pairs of headphones. And mixed in with it all, Naomi's everyday clutter – hairbrushes and nail kits and necklaces and earrings and pens.

But Bex knew there was a lot more to Naomi than was visible at a first glance – it was just a case of figuring out where to start digging.

The little desk beside the window was identical to her own: square and solid, with a couple of drawers. However, while her drawers were full of art materials and clay modelling tools, all clipped into their trays, Naomi's were full to bursting; so full that they didn't actually close. And the top of the desk? Every centimetre was covered: more jewellery, bits of paper, notebooks, screwed-up receipts, abandoned stories with black lines scored through the writing and a spaghetti of hopelessly tangled cables. The surface was littered – except for one rectangle in the middle, which was perfectly clear.

Naomi's laptop wasn't there.

"I wonder…"

Bex got down on the floor and peered under the bed. There, right at the back, a little white light blinked in the darkness.

"Just where I put mine." Bex tried not to smile.

8

Bex

Aged fourteen

"Noom? I left my geography book in…" Bex stops in the doorway of her sister's room. Naomi is halfway out of her window, one leg dangling down from the outside sill. "What are you doing?"

The look of panic on Naomi's face lasts for a couple of seconds, then vanishes. "Nothing," she says.

Bex folds her arms.

"Fine. If you *have* to know, I'm on the guest list for a gig at the Louisiana."

"You're kidding!" They've talked about the Louisiana so many times: Skinny Lister had played there, and it drove Bex crazy that their parents wouldn't let her go, or even act as chaperones for her. *Not until you're older,* they'd said. "How, though?"

"Well, you open the window and…"

"How have you got on the guest list? They're a sixteen-plus venue."

Naomi mumbles something about knowing one of the door staff.

"Take me with you!"

Naomi stares at her. "What?"

"Take me with you! You can get me in, too, right?" Bex sees her twin's hesitation and keeps going. "Come on – it'll be fun. We'll tell Mum and Dad that we're…"

"No."

"…What?"

"No."

"No, you can't get me in, or…" Bex tails off.

"No, I don't want you to come with me." Naomi turns her head away as she says it.

"Why not?"

"I just don't, OK? Jesus, Bex. It's not like we have to go everywhere together, is it? You have your friends, I have mine. These are mine, and I don't particularly want my sister tagging along." Naomi swings herself out of the window and then her head pops up. "And don't you go telling on me."

Like I'd ever tell on you, Bex thinks, bitterly.

9

Naomi

"All right, you lot. We're nearly there, so get your shit together, would you?" Ollie turned around in the driver's seat.

"What's the queue like?" croaked a voice from under a blanket.

"You can't tell from our speedy progress?"

Naomi straightened up. Her mouth tasted sour from last night's drinks and with a jolt she realized she really and truly had missed her exam. There was no going back now. Stretching herself out as best she could in the cramped van, her arm felt wrong. Her elbow was sore and she rubbed at it, thinking she must have trapped a nerve somehow.

Across from her, Ethan had woken up. He stretched his palms up to the roof of the van – and then a wide-eyed, embarrassed expression appeared on his face. It was horribly obvious that he'd forgotten all about her.

"Hey there!" She tried to keep it bright. "Did you get much sleep?"

It was no use. She could tell Ethan was thinking he'd made a huge mistake.

Sliding over the seat to the door, she heaved it open and leaned out, peering up the line of cars and vans that clogged the narrow country lane.

"OK if I get out for a minute, Ollie?" she asked.

"The traffic's been like this for the last hour. You'll be fine."

Shaking out her hair as casually as she could, she stretched against the side of the van. Naomi felt a sharp pang of regret: maybe this wasn't the smartest move, after all. At best, it was self-sabotage. At worst…

But it was too late to change her mind now.

She wondered whether Bex had even noticed she wasn't there. Bex was getting on with her life, and Naomi was living hers. Wasn't that how it was meant to be?

"So. You're coming with us, then."

It came from just behind her, from the back end of the van. It was one of the other guys from the band: the bass player. Archie? Dave? Will? Something like that.

"Ethan said you had a spare pass, so he asked me along."

"You know it's his girlfriend's, right? That doesn't bother you?"

Naomi laughed. "I don't want to be his girlfriend. I'm just coming for the music. That's all."

"That's what they all say, darlin'." Archie-Dave-Will

turned away and swung the back door open, climbing inside and slamming it behind him.

"Wanker," she muttered under her breath.

She peered at herself in the wing mirror. She had looked better, but given that she'd only had a couple of hours' sleep in a van, it could be worse. She needed to get some water into her system as soon as they got to the festival site. And some food, too…

She was really doing it. Nobody here knew anything about her – other than what she told them. She could be anyone she wanted. Ordinary Naomi – the one with the twin and the exams and the parents – could simply blow away on the wind. It was complete, anonymous freedom.

"Looks like we're moving! All aboard," shouted Ollie, and Naomi swung herself back into the van, slamming the door after her.

The conversation stopped abruptly and Ethan glared at her. She decided not to notice and gave him a dazzling smile.

"Are you nervous, then?" she asked.

"Nervous?"

"You know, about your set. It's all feeling pretty real now, I guess?"

"We've done this set, like, a hundred times before."

"They say festivals are always different, though, don't they?"

"Who says that?"

She shrugged. "Just bands I've spoken to. And friends."

"Which bands?"

"Nobody huge or anything – guys who play lots of festivals."

Ethan narrowed his eyes at her. "Every show's different." He turned away – their conversation was obviously over.

They inched forwards as the rolling roadblock of festival traffic crept on. Three cars ahead, one guy had climbed on to the roof of the car and was clinging to the top with a wide grin. Other cars had stuck flags and banners out of their windows, like they had all decided to start the party early. A drone whizzed overhead and disappeared off up the queue.

The road ahead of them gradually cleared and stewards waved the van on as Ollie steered around potholes and puddles, and then, right in front of them, the road ended at a tall, solid fence and a gate manned by two security guards in hi-vis. "Here we are, gents … and lady," Ollie said. "Hemisphere."

"Mind your backs!" Ollie dragged the bass drum out of the van. "Naomi? Can you chuck that pedal over to me? The one by your feet." He rested the drum against his ribs and pointed with his free hand.

Naomi grabbed it and held it out to him. "You want me to carry this for you? I don't mind – you look pretty laden down."

"Nah. It's fine, really. Thanks for the offer, though – it's more than this lot have ever done." Laughing, he took the drum pedal from her. "Right. Better go get checked in."

All around them, vans were unloading: there were shouts and clangs of instruments and mic stands being hauled out of vehicles and stacked on to trolleys. On the far side of the field, a row of tour buses with blacked-out windows sat in the middle of a huddle of roadies – and in between all of them, runners and festival staff were bustling about with clipboards and boxes. A woman with hair dyed turquoise and purple with streaks of pink stopped alongside the van and peered at the list she was carrying.

"Are you Parrish?" she asked.

Ethan shoved his way through the others. "Parrish? That's us. I'm Ethan, the singer. Nice to meet you…" His eyes flicked down to the lanyard around her neck and back up again. "Ellie."

Ellie barely even looked at him as she ticked off a line on her clipboard and scribbled a quick note. "Well, Evan, was it?"

"Ethan."

"Right. Sure. I need you to come straight to the

backstage office to finish the paperwork. We messengered your passes yesterday, right?" Her eyes flicked up to survey the band's lanyards. "Make sure they're visible at all times, please. You can bring your kit over now and leave it in area B." Again, her eyes skimmed the group, then came to rest on Naomi. "You the manager?"

"No!" Naomi shook her head, trying to ignore Ethan's snort.

He stepped right in front of her. "She's just a friend. I'm in charge of the band."

"Five minutes," Ellie said clearly.

"Sure thing." He flashed her the smile again – and this time, she glanced up in time to catch it. The eye-roll she gave him was probably not what he was hoping for.

"Seriously. Get that paperwork signed or you'll lose your slot." She clipped her pen back on to her staff lanyard and was gone.

"Do we need ID? Shit. I've only got my uni card," muttered Archie-Dave-Will. The keyboard player slapped his back in mock-pity, and as one they turned to stare at the pile of instruments, cables, stands and microphones.

Once the band had hefted all their kit in the direction Ellie had sent them, Naomi leaned back against the van. She needed a plan – put her wellies on, put her trainers in her bag and put the bag back in the van.

Except the van was locked.

And Ollie had walked off with the key.

Naomi swore quietly to herself as she hopped from one foot to the other, trying to swap her trainers for her wellies without putting either foot down in the mud. She stuffed her trainers into the outside pocket of the bag.

"Hey! You! Girl by the van!" A security guard in a hi-vis jacket was peering at her. "Where's your wristband?"

"I have a pass…?" She tugged out the lanyard from under her jacket.

The guard strode over. "I need to check your wristband."

"Oh. My … my boyfriend must still have it. He's just gone through…"

"The lanyard is for access to the backstage area only. You'll need a wristband for the main site. Go to the office and show them your pass, tell them you've lost the wristband and you need a new one." He jerked his thumb behind him, in the opposite direction to the way the band had gone.

"Oh. OK. Thank you!" She gave him a bright smile as he walked off.

Ethan hadn't mentioned a wristband.

Another band, a trio dragging a trolley loaded up with kit hurried past – and at the exact moment they crossed behind the van, the trolley tipped, spilling their equipment with a deafening crash.

The noise made her head spin – she clamped her hands

over her ears, trying to block out the sound. Without warning, an image of Bex flashed through her mind but Naomi pushed it aside. When they were little, they'd known what the other was thinking without needing to ask. If one of them got sick, the other did, too. Their parents had put that down to the amount of time they spent together ... but Naomi knew it was more than that. Trying to find the words to explain it was like trying to describe how breathing feels.

Every time she thought back over how things used to be, Naomi was sure Bex must remember it, too. How could she not?

Naomi traipsed over to the office the guard had pointed out and joined the back of the queue. One by one, they shuffled forwards. Her turn came and she held out a hand as a girl wrapped a fabric band tightly around her wrist. A heavy clamp swung down, snapping the wristband firmly shut. Tugging at it to loosen it a little, she headed back towards the security gate and into the backstage area.

10

Naomi

Aged eleven

The sun is still hot for September as Naomi heads for the school field. After three weeks, the sprawl of school buildings are starting to feel familiar – yesterday she even managed to find the drama studio on her first attempt … which meant that she was actually on time for a change.

Not that Bex had noticed: she had walked in two minutes later, arm in arm with Kay, and sat down on the front bench without even acknowledging her. Naomi had picked up her bag and climbed over the three benches in between them, and dropped on to the seat on the other side of Bex. Her sister and Kay had carried on their conversation while she sat there, waiting for them to finish. She'd put her bag on her lap and rummaged through it like she was looking for something…

For the last couple of weeks, it had been hard getting Bex to notice she was there at all.

They didn't finish each other's sentences any more. And she couldn't feel Bex in her head as she drifted off to sleep. It would be OK; Naomi was sure it would. They were

Bex-and-Naomi, Naomi-and-Bex. They knew each other better than anyone ever could – nothing could change that.

Not even Kay.

She flicks a late-summer fly off the rolled-up sleeve of her school shirt, throwing herself down on the grass in the shade of the huge chestnut tree. It's become her favourite place to spend lunchtime. She leans her head back against the trunk of the tree and closes her eyes, letting the sounds of the school wash over her.

"There you are – I've been looking for you everywhere!"

Naomi opens one eye.

Kay is standing in the sun, her shirt so bright in the light that it hurts to look at her, even when Naomi shades her eyes with her hand.

"Looking for me? Why?"

"Because we were supposed to meet right after the bell, remember?"

"We were?"

"I knew you weren't listening to me in Spanish! I said I wanted to talk to you about something?"

She thinks I'm Bex.

Naomi is about to tell Kay she's got the wrong twin ... but as she opens her mouth, Kay lowers her voice.

"It's about your sister, OK?"

Naomi closes her mouth.

"Look, I know you two are super close, and she's your twin…"

But…?

"But I just…" Kay pokes at something on the ground with the toe of her shoe. "I just like it better when it's the two of us. Without Naomi."

"Without. Naomi."

"I know. I'm sorry. But it's easier with two, right? And I don't want to make her feel bad, but, well, best friends don't come in threes…"

What would Bex say now? Naomi wonders. *Would she say anything?*

Naomi looks at Kay, and Kay looks at Naomi and sees only Bex.

"And anyway," Kay adds with a winning smile, "it's like you said – sometimes, your sister's just a bit *weird.*"

11

Bex

There was nothing in Naomi's email. Or rather, there was *plenty* in Naomi's email – all of it useless. Bex cracked the password on her second try – it was 'Brutus', the name of the hamster they'd had when they were kids. Naomi had insisted on naming the poor thing: she was in the middle of her acting phase at the time.

There were a couple of messages about the creative writing group Naomi went to every Thursday night, and Bex skimmed through the most recent but there was nothing that looked like it was going to help. It was just a thread of complaints about a deadline they'd been set by the group leader. Somehow, none of those people felt like the kind Naomi would run away with.

Facebook was next, and Bex scanned the feed. It was mostly updates from pages Naomi had 'liked', a few people from school and one or two from the writing group. Nothing jumped out at her. It was all very … normal.

All very … boring.

I'm missing something, she thought. *I just don't know what it is.*

Holding out one last hope, she clicked on the private message inbox. The most recent was from Simeon.

Bex skimmed through it and immediately wished she hadn't. It was a break-up message and it managed to be both bland and utterly crushing at the same time; telling Naomi that she was shallow, that she wasn't who he had thought she would be.

Naomi had never been particularly into sharing when it came to talking about Simeon but when she *did* mention him, her sister had made him sound like he was a reasonably nice guy. Reading his message, on the other hand…

If that's what you think a nice guy is, who the hell else are you hanging out with, Noom?

She resisted the urge to send Simeon a message of her own, and clicked back to Naomi's main page and started typing. The post was small and simple and to the point.

Hi. This is Bex, Naomi's twin. My sister has been missing since last night. She left a message saying she's with friends but we can't reach her. It probably doesn't sound like a big deal, but she also missed her final GCSE paper, and that's not like her. If you've seen her or she's with you, please please please can you ask her to get in touch so we know she's safe. And Naomi, if you're reading this somewhere: call me. Please.

She read it through once more, added her phone number and hit 'Post'.

A part of her wanted to stare at the screen, just in case someone replied. But the longer she stared at it, the darker the shadow of doubt in her mind became.

Nobody replied. Everybody from their year at school would be getting ready for the party. She clicked idly through the browser history – it was mostly her social sites and a couple of gossip pages.

I'm missing something.

Resting her head against the edge of Naomi's bed, she stared at the pictures and posters on the walls. There were a few band posters, a handful of adverts torn out of magazines and some pictures from a couple of TV shows. A few photos of the two of them, a couple of them with their parents. Black-and-white postcards of city views: New York, Paris, London. A moody, full-page portrait of Liam Neeson – also torn out of a magazine. Despite everything, Bex smiled. She had never understood her sister's lifelong devotion to him – he was *old*, for a start.

The room felt like Naomi.

That Facebook page … didn't.

Every time I come in here, she's on her laptop but she shuts it before I get too close.

She has another Facebook account.

Bex picked a link in the browser history at random

and clicked on it.

You must be logged in to view this page.

"Oh, come on!" Bex smacked the side of the screen. If Naomi had used her real name for her other account, this one could be anything.

She glared at the login page. "I know you. I *know* I know you."

Bex made herself dissolve. It wasn't her sitting on the floor in Naomi's room, it was Naomi. Naomi who had come home and opened her laptop like it was any other day, any normal day. She was sitting on the floor and she was typing…

Bex let her mind empty. And her fingers started to move.

She had no idea what she'd actually typed – it could have been anything. Anything at all. She hit the 'Enter' key – and it worked.

Bex was too pleased to even be surprised.

If the other Facebook page had been quiet, this one was seriously loud. The feed was jammed with photos, posts and updates: groups of people hugging, making faces at the camera. There were shots of parties, huge crowds in the background and friends holding up half-empty bottles of Jack Daniels or shot glasses, shouting into the camera lens. An unfamiliar band onstage, sweat dripping off them. A close-up of someone playing a bass guitar, winking at the camera. Naomi, her head thrown back to balance an upside-down shot glass on her chin.

There were endless posts directly to Naomi – how was she feeling after a 'big night', how good it had been to party with her, was she going to this gig or that gig and did she know how to get backstage for some band or another...?

Bex didn't recognize a single one of the names or faces. This Naomi had over a thousand friends – and all of them looked older than her and Naomi. But in the photos, Naomi looked older herself. She was dressed differently, she even stood differently. In one, she had her arms around a guy and a girl, posing like they were her best friends in the world, all wearing brightly coloured wigs and neon-yellow T-shirts.

It was the profile picture that bothered Bex the most. In it, Naomi was wearing sunglasses and posing against a graffiti-covered wall. There was no sign of the sister she knew.

Or thought she knew.

This new Naomi claimed she was eighteen, that she was an undergraduate at Bristol University and worked at the student radio station.

She posted the same message on the new wall but she added a single line at the end.

PS My sister is FIFTEEN.

She watched the post slide on to the screen and closed

the laptop, setting it gently on the desk as her head spun.

Had she let Naomi down by not being there?

"Who are you, Naomi?"

Bex stayed in Naomi's room. It felt like the right place to be. She lost count of the number of times she tried Naomi's mobile. It was hopeless.

Needed some time.

Time? For what?

Propped up on the top of the chest of drawers was a photo of Naomi – this one in a frame. It was Naomi in her first school play. Bex smiled at the memory. Naomi had been so determined she was going to be an actor … and then she'd completely forgotten all her lines.

Fear and embarrassment, and wishing the ground would open up and swallow her, just so it could all be over.

She remembered feeling it, sitting in the auditorium. It was only Bex who had known how Naomi *really* felt. As soon as it was over, Bex had slipped out of her seat and run through the hall, all the way round to the classroom that was being used as a dressing room, and when she got to Naomi, she'd thrown her arms around her while her twin sobbed into her shoulder.

I felt it. I felt it like it was me.

A stack of paper beside the chest of drawers slid over and

sheets slipped across the floor. Revision notes, pages torn out of notebooks. Endless pieces of stories or critiques from Naomi's writing group. Nothing that looked like it would help right now.

She peered into the desk drawers. More paper. A few pens, most of them without lids. A lipstick. A handful of change...

Where was the money?

Bex shuffled everything in the drawers from side to side. Naomi kept her money in the drawer on the left. She always had.

No. No money.

What else wasn't there? Bex opened the wardrobe and peered in. Jumpers, jeans, at least eight pairs of denim shorts. Band shirts.

Right at the back of the wardrobe, under a basket of shoes, there was a small, lidded cardboard box that Bex had never seen before. She slid it out and sat with it on her lap, half afraid to open it.

It was full of ticket stubs. Gig tickets, wristbands, backstage passes and lanyards. Scribbled notes and phone numbers on the back of beer mats; a handful of retro Polaroid-style photos. They were of Naomi and a curly haired guy wearing a Star Wars stormtrooper costume, the helmet tucked under his arm as he clutched a pair of drumsticks. It had a scribbled message at the bottom, signed with a looping 'S'.

For a while, Bex sat on the floor with her head in her hands, surrounded by the sea of Naomi's secrets. She had never felt so alone.

Or so betrayed.

Bex snatched up a handful of tickets and threw them across the room with a scream of frustrated rage. Then she threw the pillow as hard as she could at the wall. It caught the necklaces and the photo of Naomi and Simeon and took them down with it. Feet slipping on paper, Bex turned towards the desk ... and stopped. In the place where Naomi's pillow had been, there was a photo.

It was a photo of them, laughing. Their dad had taken it on holiday three years ago, the summer there had been a heatwave and ants had invaded their tent. They'd spent the whole ten days in the campsite pool: it was too hot to do anything else, and it was – thinking about it – the last time she remembered seeing Naomi smile like that.

She pressed her hands to her forehead but it didn't help. It was like steam pouring from a kettle, building and building and building until it was a boiling cloud. A high-pitched whining filled her ears – and suddenly, cutting through it, there was a deafening crash that somehow came from everywhere and just the middle of her head simultaneously.

"Ow. Ow. Ow."

She clutched her head, her fingers digging into her scalp and then, as abruptly as it had started, it was *gone*.

Bex lowered her hands slowly, as though moving too fast would bring it right back again. Nothing.

"Rebecca?" Her dad's voice was calling from the hall. "We're going to go down to the police station. Coming?"

Bex closed Naomi's laptop and slid it back into its hiding place, then kicked the worst of the mess she'd made under the bed.

⚘

The corridor of the police station smelled like bleach. Her parents had been in one of the offices for what felt like hours, but which the giant clock on the wall stubbornly told her had only been forty-five minutes. The police had spoken to her first. The questions were so obvious that Bex didn't see the point … but she answered them.

Whichever way she came at it, however she tried to consider it, Bex always worked her way round to the same answer.

I let her down.

Bex eyed the vending machine on the other side of the corridor, where a cute guy with freckles, in a checked shirt and beaten-up jeans was standing, picking up a cup from the dispensing slot. He turned away, blowing on the surface of his drink, and started to walk down the corridor to an interview room with an open door. Who was he? Why was he there?

Horrified, she saw him stop and turn to look right at her before smiling and carrying on the way he'd been going.

She felt her cheeks burning and shrank as far back into her seat as she could. But maybe coffee wasn't a bad idea, so with a sigh, she unfolded herself from the hard plastic chair and went over to the machine, then fed a handful of change from her pocket into the slot. She dropped in the last twenty pence piece.

The machine threw it back out.

She put it back in again.

It hurled it back out.

This time, she shoved the coin in so hard that it jammed.

"Stupid machine," she muttered. "Stupid, stupid, *stupid* thing! Why won't you just *work?*"

She was hitting the drinks dispenser with the flat of her hand – loud and hard enough to make the woman sitting further down the corridor and knitting, look up at her.

"Hey. Hey," said an unfamiliar voice, and a hand slid in between hers and the plastic. "You should watch out. If you provoke them, they can bite – vicious things when they're cornered, drinks dispensers."

Bex took a step back.

It was the guy in the checked shirt, and he was looking at her with undisguised concern in his hazel eyes.

"This is almost certainly a stupid question, so I'm sorry – but … are you OK?" he asked. "No. You're right. It's definitely a stupid question. You're not OK. Nobody decides to wrestle a vending machine when they're OK. Unless that's your hobby or something – in which case, this just got weird." He cocked his head on one side. "*Are* you a part-time vending machine wrestler?"

For the first time that morning, Bex laughed. She couldn't not. But then she couldn't stop laughing; even when she tried.

I am not going to cry.

She just about managed to get "I think the machine hates me" out.

"I think the machine hates everyone," he said. "I'm Joshua. Josh. I don't know why I said Joshua. Nobody calls me Joshua. Except my grandmother, and she's dead." He blinked at her.

"You have literally no filter, do you?"

"No. I don't." He looked completely serious.

"I'm Bex. Short for Rebecca."

"Not Becky."

"Not if I can help it."

"I'm the same. Funny about what people call me, I mean. Not that I wouldn't like being called Becky … although that would be interesting, wouldn't it?"

Literally. No. Filter.

It was kind of sweet.

Bex looked him up and down. "I'd say you were more of an Elizabeth."

"Here." He held out his cup of coffee. "Take mine. I've not had any yet, I promise – it's too hot. But you look like you need it more than I do."

"My sister. She's missing." Bex hadn't meant to say it but it just sort of … fell out.

"Oh. Shit. Sorry." Josh stared at the floor. "Actually…" He looked back up and cocked his head on one side. "I've had coffee from this thing before. It's *always* horrible. If you want a decent cup, there's a café across the road…?" He left the question hanging.

Bex cleared her throat.

"Well," said Josh. "This is awkward." He shrugged. "I get it, I do – a complete stranger interrupts your one-woman battle against the machines and asks you to go for coffee. I'd have that exact same look on my face, too. It's just … I know how it feels to be sitting here for hours with … this." He held up the little polystyrene cup to demonstrate his point. "And it looked like you could use someone to talk to. But I made it weird, so I'm going to go now. Take it." He pressed the cup into her hand. "I swear I've not spat in it. But if you change your mind, I'll be in the café with the green sign. At least until my dad finally convinces my grandad that we're here to take him home. Which will probably take a while." He smiled. "It was nice to meet you, Bex. I hope it all works out all right with your sister."

And he turned and started to walk off down the corridor.

Bex looked at the cup of coffee in her hand then sniffed it cautiously. It smelled revolting. She took a tiny sip. It didn't taste any better than it smelled.

Coffee sounded nice. Real coffee.

She looked back down the corridor to the office where her parents were. The door was still shut.

The lady paused from her knitting and looked up.

"If my parents come out, can you tell them I went to the café over the road?"

Knitting Lady shrugged, then nodded and carried on.

"Thanks." Bex lobbed the plastic cup into the bin beside the machine and hurried down the corridor to catch up with Josh. "Hey! Josh? Actually, a coffee sounds really good…"

He stopped and looked round. "You tried it, didn't you?"

"How do they make it taste *so* bad?"

"Science. Come on – the café's great."

12

Naomi

This is more like it, thought Naomi. She was finally backstage at a music festival. But even travelling light, she was tired and her bag had started to feel heavier and heavier, making her back and shoulders ache. She wasn't going to start her time at Hemisphere like that, so she stashed her bag carefully behind a row of large road cases just inside the gate. It should be safe there for a few minutes, she thought. That done, she stood in the middle of the security-screened area, willing herself to take it all in. Runners with headsets were rushing from one place to another, journalists and photographers loitered and checked their phones. In one corner, someone from a TV station was trying to interview two members of The Flip Flops. Outside another Portakabin, the lead singer from Tudor Rose was changing her shoes, while another band that Naomi vaguely recognized were chatting to the drummer from Dreadnought Fury.

It was almost a shock to remember that she should have been sitting an exam that morning. It felt like another life already. A skin she had shed – along with

Simeon. Along with Bex.

She stepped out of the way of a runner shooing Darkling Mirror along to wherever they were supposed to be, followed by a publicist shouting into a phone and wondered, *Why can't I stay as this Naomi?*

She'd written a couple of gig reviews before, hadn't she? What if that was her thing, just like Bex had her art? All their lives, Bex had been so confident that art was what she wanted to do, what she was *meant* to do. What if this was her turn?

"Hey, man. You got a light?" A tall guy in skinny black jeans and a ripped vintage Ramones shirt was standing by her.

"No, sorry. Don't smoke," she said with a shrug.

"You with the festival, or…" He waved a hand vaguely.

"I'm here with a couple of friends – they're in Parrish. They had a spare pass, so…" She noticed his expression shift slightly and he sniffed.

"Their drummer, he's cool. Great snare work. But the singer? He's a douche, man." And with that, he wandered off.

She put it out of her mind. Ethan didn't matter. This – the electricity of being backstage, this was what life was about. Not sitting in a stupid exam room. This was real.

It was still only Friday and Hemisphere may not have been Glastonbury but it was big enough. It felt like she had finally come home.

Smiling, she turned back towards the stack of road cases

with an idea: seeing as she was already backstage, she could take some photos – maybe even snatch a couple of interviews. She had a lanyard and her phone. It was perfect. Naomi clambered over the pile of cables at the side of the road cases and reached for her bag...

The bag was gone.

At first, she thought she must have made a mistake – but there were no other piles of cases. Ducking back out from behind the cases, she looked around. Nobody seemed to be acting suspiciously and no one was obviously walking off with her stuff.

"Shit."

Everything was in her bag. Most of her cash. Her phone. Everything.

She spotted a steward walking past and broke into a run.

"Hi! Hello? Excuse me? I need some help."

"Hmm?"

"I had a bag and I put it down for a minute. It's gone. It's just gone!"

"Has someone you know picked it up for you?"

"No. I think it's been stolen."

"You need to report it at the main security desk in the middle of the site."

As she weaved her way towards security, following the steward's directions, the sounds (and smells) of the main field came closer. Cigarettes, beer, burgers, sun cream, sweat. Laughter. Shouting. The occasional scream – punctuated by a repeated "One. One-two. One-two-one…" of a roadie testing a mic.

After the organized chaos of backstage, being out in the main site was a shock. There were people everywhere. She was dazzled by it, trying to absorb it all … and then a girl wearing her T-shirt walked right in front of her.

"Hey!"

Naomi lunged forwards and grabbed the girl's shoulder. "Where did you get that?"

The girl glared at her. "Get your hand off me."

"Where did you get that shirt?" Naomi jabbed at the swirling design across the front of the T-shirt. It was a one-of-a-kind shirt: Bex had made it for her as a gift. It had been funny, in a way: she'd given Bex a T-shirt with her favourite sculpture on it, Bex had given her a T-shirt she'd painted at the craft shop in town. Neither of them had told the other what they'd been planning. "That's my shirt," Naomi said.

"I don't think so."

"Yes. It is. It was in my bag. Which – interestingly – I was just about to report stolen…" Naomi would have said more – she was just getting into her stride – but she stopped as someone else came over. It was a short, stocky man much older than she was, with close-cropped hair and a sunburnt neck. He stopped beside the girl and wrapped an arm round her shoulder.

"Problem?" he asked.

Naomi looked from the girl to the guy, and then back again.

He frowned, tipped his head on one side and said, "I *said*, is there a problem?"

Naomi shook her head in frustration. She knew how it worked: a bag went missing and its contents got scattered. She couldn't prove anything. "Whatever," she said – and was about to walk away when the guy's back pocket started ringing … with her phone ring.

"Seriously?" She stared at him. "You've got my phone?"

"No," he said.

"That's my ringtone."

"Funny coincidence."

"Look, you've got my T-shirt and you've got my phone. Just give me my stuff back, please?" Then Naomi realized the two of them had stepped apart from one another and had cut her off against the fence… She took a step backwards and found her spine pressed against the chainlink of one of the fences.

The girl suddenly spotted the lanyard around her neck. Even as Naomi tried to turn away, a hand snapped forward and yanked down on the lanyard so hard that the strap broke.

"Hey! You can't take that!" Naomi shouted, trying to grab it back – but the man shoved her against the fence and kept her pinned there.

"Please – I need that!" she begged but all the two of them did was smirk.

"Hey!" A man's voice came from behind the others. Startled, the couple bolted, leaving Naomi slumped against the fence with her heart pounding.

"You OK?" the man asked.

"I'm fine. Thanks."

"No problem – but if you don't mind me saying, you don't look fine."

She sighed. "They took my stuff."

"Shit. Sorry."

"Yeah, well." Naomi's hands were shaking and her knees felt like they were full of water.

"I'm Max," the guy said.

"Naomi." She gave him a wobbly smile and he smiled back.

He had a nice smile, she thought, which dimpled the corners of his mouth. His hair was a sort of mousy brown, pushed back from his forehead by a pair of designer sunglasses – and he was wearing possibly the least practical clothes she'd ever seen for a festival: a pristine white shirt, khakis and deck shoes and an expensive-looking rucksack slung carelessly over his shoulder.

"You need something?" he asked.

She shook her head. "No. Thanks, but I'm OK. I was just heading to security. My whole bag went, so…"

"Is that it?" Max pointed to something that had been half stuffed into one of the recycling bins, wedging the lid open.

With a yelp, she dodged past Max and rushed over to the bin, yanking the lid open and snatching her bag. Everything was gone except for the blue wig, which she pulled out and dusted off gloomily then stuffed the bag back into the bin.

"Well, at least they left this," she muttered, brandishing it. "Everything else has gone. They even took my backstage pass – can you believe that?"

"Dicks," said Max. "I'll walk you over to security."

"No." It came out more sharply than she'd meant it to, but she was already having trouble keeping herself from crying. She needed to use the walk over to the office to pull herself together, report her bag stolen, get a replacement lanyard and go straight backstage again until she felt calmer. "No, thanks. Honestly. You helped already. It's OK – I'll be fine."

He studied her. "You promise?"

"I promise."

"Well, if you're sure." He shrugged then slipped his backpack off his shoulder and tugged it open. "But take this – if you've lost all your stuff, it's the least I can do…" He held out a fleecy hoodie.

"I can't take that! What if you need it?"

"Give it to me when you see me again."

"What makes you think I'll see you again?"

"Oh, I don't know. Maybe I'm just hoping..." He swung his bag back on to his shoulder. "I'll see you," he called back.

13

Bex

The café *was* nice. It was bright and welcoming, with a blackboard listing a dozen different types of tea and coffee hanging on the bare brick wall behind the counter. There were armchairs dotted around small, low wooden tables and the radio playing quietly in the background.

"See what I mean?" Josh said as they settled into a pair of chairs beside the window – Bex keeping one eye on the entrance to the station in case her parents emerged. "I always feel better coming here." He blew on the surface of his coffee and took a sip. He seemed to be waiting for her to say something.

"You said you come when your dad's in the police station?"

"Yeah." He nodded and his sunny expression darkened a little. "My grandad, he has dementia. He gets lost."

"Oh. I'm sorry." She fiddled with the edge of her cup, feeling clumsy and rude.

"It's kind of normal now, you know? Every couple of weeks, he just goes off. He thinks he's going to meet my grandma for their first date. 'Walking out,' he calls it. He forgets that she's gone, and that he's got a dodgy hip and a couple of kids and grandkids and he just … goes." Josh ran a hand through his hair. "We know where to look for him most of the time – he goes to the park where they met. But sometimes he's not there. And then we have to call the police. Hence…" He waved a hand at the window.

"Wow. That must be hard."

"No harder than what you're going through. I think Dad's getting more worried about it than he used to, though." Josh's voice got quieter and Bex realized that he didn't want to talk about his grandfather any more than she wanted to talk about Naomi.

"So," she said as brightly as she could, "do they do food here?"

"There's cakes…"

The last thing she'd eaten was a bowl of marshmallow cereal at Kay's but cake was probably better than nothing.

"Cake sounds great," she began – and before she could say anything else, Josh had bounced up from his seat and over to the counter. In no time at all, he was bouncing right back over carrying a plate with five different slices on it.

"I got a couple," he said.

"A couple?" Bex raised an eyebrow.

"They're really good. And I could say we were sharing,

so she wouldn't judge me."

"Are we sharing?"

"Mmfffaanntt phhhmbfff." Josh's mouth was already full of cake.

Trying not to laugh, Bex broke a corner off a slice of speckled sponge cake.

"I like your T-shirt," he said, swallowing his mouthful. "It's Patricia Volk, isn't it?"

"Wow! You know her? She's one of my favourite artists – I can't believe you recognized it!"

"I spotted it back in the station. But I couldn't exactly say anything then, because then I'd be going up to a complete stranger and telling them I'd been staring at their … umm, yeah."

"But now we're not complete strangers, so it's OK?"

"Of course. We've shared cake. Anything goes now." He brushed a couple of crumbs off the edge of the table.

"So … how come you know about Patricia Volk?"

"I love her work!" He visibly brightened again. "I'm applying to art school for autumn next year."

"Seriously?"

"Well … yeah."

"It's just – that's what I'm going to do. The year after, though."

"Really? Where are you looking?"

"I was thinking about sculpture at Glasgow School of Art."

"I went to their open day for the environmental art course!" He shook his head. "Talk about a coincidence, right? That's amazing! We could be at the same uni in a couple of years! What kind of sculpture?" he asked, and when she looked blank he added, "Like, I want to make public art, you know? Stuff that's out there for everyone to see. Not stuck in a gallery or something."

Bex had never really considered that someone chose to make that kind of art. She'd always thought it was more like wallpaper: you bought it from catalogues or big warehouses on industrial estates. "As in, 'I'll meet you by the giant bronze guy with the suitcase on the main concourse at three o'clock' kind of art?"

A frown clouded his face. "It's still art, you know. It's there for people to look at, making the world a bit better, even if it's not on a nice little plinth with a price tag."

"That's not what I meant!" Bex realized she sounded like a complete snob. "I'd just not really thought about it. I'm sorry. You're right."

"It's fine. I didn't mean to get all intense on you." He gulped down another mouthful of cake. "But you're meant to be telling me about your stuff, right? What do you want to make?"

Bex let out a long, thoughtful breath. "I've made lots of pieces at school but they never come out looking the way they do in my head. And Naomi – my sister – she always squints at them and asks me whether I meant them to look like a squashed dog with a pot on top of it, or a banana with horse legs." She smiled as she said it. Naomi would come up with ever-more ridiculous ways of describing the things Bex made. It was a double-act of Bex's art and Naomi's words: probably the closest they came to deliberately doing anything together any more.

She suddenly wanted to tell Josh about Naomi ... but the cake had done nothing to help her head. If anything, the sugar and the caffeine between them had made the feeling of fingers tapping on the inside of her brain worse. It was like a migraine, but different. There was pressure on the inside of her skull and the outside, and every hair on the back of her neck stood up, one at a time.

Bex rubbed her forehead, hoping it would stop. It didn't. Everything felt foggy.

"Is somebody smoking in here?"

"Huh?"

"There's... It's like smoke. Smoke and ... I don't know."

"There's only us in here. Look." He waved a hand around.

"But I can..." She looked around. He was right: all the other chairs were empty but the smell of smoke remained. "You really can't...? Nothing?"

Bex slumped back in her chair, her head in her hands. "I'm sorry," she said from between her fingers. "I think..."

I need to go home."

"Your phone's ringing," Josh said gently and nudged her jacket, which was balled up on the seat beside her.

She scrabbled through her pockets to find it. "Hello?"

"Sweetheart, we're finished here for now. Where are you?"

"I'm in the café over the road…"

"Are you all right? You sound a little strange."

"I'm fine. I have a headache, but…"

"Wait right there. We'll come and get you."

"No, you go. I'm fine, I promise. I think I need some air. I'm going to finish my coffee and I'll walk."

"Are you sure? If you're not feeling well."

"It's OK, Mum. I've got…" She paused and glanced up at Josh – hoovering up the last of the cake crumbs – "I've got a friend with me."

In his seat across from her, Josh waited until she put her phone away, then shuffled awkwardly in his seat.

"So, you … you, umm … said your sister was missing? Was there any news?"

"That was just my mum saying they're going home." Bex sighed. "Her name's Naomi. My sister, not my mum. Obviously. She's my twin. She… I don't know. She didn't turn up for our exam this morning and that's all they know. Looks like she's run away. She left a note saying she was with friends, but that's all. Not who, not what she's doing, not where she's going. Nothing."

"All *they* know?" He repeated her words back to her, emphasizing the *they*.

"I meant all *we* know."

"Look. I know it's none of my business and I know we've only just met – but if you wanted to talk to someone … I'm here. And I'm a good listener."

"You are?"

"Allegedly." He looked suddenly uncomfortable. "All I'm saying is that sometimes it helps to talk to someone who's not involved. Maybe it's not so bad…?"

"She ditched her last GCSE and nobody knows where she is or why," Bex snapped, glaring at him. "She took some cash, but that's about it. And I was looking in her room – just looking, for … I don't even know. But she had this whole secret life pretending to be somebody else. And I don't know who that is, and I'm not even sure I know who *she* is any more. So yeah, it *is* so bad, actually."

Josh blinked at her, apparently lost for an answer. Time slowed to a crawl and eventually he frowned, sighed and opened his mouth.

"Maybe she just didn't want to sit the exam."

Bex laughed coldly. "You don't know Naomi."

"Well, don't take this the wrong way," he said, knitting his fingers together around his knees, "but maybe you don't, either. At least, not as well as you think you do."

There was no answer to that and they both knew it.

The silence stretched between them until Bex couldn't take it any more.

"I'm sorry," she said. "I think I had some kind of weird panic attack before. I'm not normally like this."

He waved her apology away. "I'm sorry, too. I sounded like a right prick then, didn't I? I'm not – I promise."

"You mean you just manage to *sound* like one?"

"Only on Tuesdays, Thursdays and around girls I think I could maybe like."

"But it's Friday. Oh." She could feel her cheeks burning, and was almost relieved to see that he had also turned scarlet.

"That probably came out wrong."

"Yes. No. *Yes*, actually. But in kind of a *nice* way?"

"I'll take that." He stood up – still blushing – and brushed an incredible amount of crumbs from his jeans. "I didn't mean to listen in… But I heard you saying you wanted to walk home. Would I be making this whole thing even weirder if I said I didn't really think that's a great idea if you're having panic attacks? What I'm saying," he continued, "is that – only if you wanted – I could walk you back? No more weirdness, I swear. You don't even have to talk to me if you don't want to. I'd just feel better knowing you got back OK."

"I think," she said, slipping her jacket on as she stood,

"that the not-talking would definitely make it weirder. But apart from that … it sounds good. Thank you." An idea suddenly struck her. "But don't you have to… Your family…?"

"One sec." He pulled his phone out of his pocket. Bex tried not to smile when she saw him sticking the tip of his tongue out of the corner of his mouth as he typed. "There." He dropped his phone back into his pocket. "I've told Dad I'll find my own way home. So. Which way's home?"

"That way." She nodded down the street. "I just have to get my bag…" Bex looked under the seat. There was nothing there: just a scattering of crumbs on the otherwise clear floor.

"Your bag?" Josh sounded puzzled. He stepped away from the door, letting it close again.

"Yeah, my bag. It was right … here…" She looked under the table, under the chair Josh had been sitting in. It was impossible: her bag had gone, and yet they had been alone in the café the whole time. "I can't go without my bag!" She was trying to stay calm, but the panic was rising through her chest, up into her throat and out of her mouth. "It's got all my…"

"Bex?" Josh's voice was quiet but firm. "Bex. You didn't *have* a bag."

"I … what?" She didn't have a bag with her. She'd been

so sure… "Oh … no. I didn't, did I?"

"I mean – unless you left it at the police station…? Maybe you did that?"

Bex pressed the heels of her hands into her eye sockets. "I'm an idiot. Sorry. No bag. I'm *so* embarrassed!"

"Hey … hey." Josh's hand touched her elbow. "Don't be. You're allowed to be stressed out."

He opened the door again and held it for her to walk through, hopping down on to the pavement behind her and standing there with his hands in his pockets.

She started walking and he fell into step alongside her.

"Has your sister done this before?" Josh ducked around the bus stop and back on to the pavement. He moved so easily, so comfortably. Even though she'd only just met him, he made everything feel almost normal.

"Not like this. Naomi… She messes around, and she sneaks out when she thinks nobody knows … and I kept it a secret because that's what twins are meant to do, isn't it? We're meant to look out for each other. Today I found all these tickets in her room and it hit me. She has this whole other *life*. She even has a separate Facebook account, too."

"What did your mum and dad say when you told them?"

"Hmm?" She was so lost in her own thoughts that she'd only been half listening.

"Your mum and dad. What did they say?"

"I … haven't told them?" Even as Bex said it, she knew

102

how bad it sounded.

"You haven't told them? But you told the police about it, right?"

"Noooo…?" Bex shook her head. That didn't sound any better, either.

Josh stopped walking and stared at her. "How come?"

"Because I…" She stopped. "I…" How was she supposed to explain it? "Because," she managed eventually, "I don't know what they'll say. Or do."

What Bex didn't say was that part of her was afraid their parents would blame her. That they would either assume she must have known or blame her for *not* having known.

And what about Naomi? What would she think?

"And I suppose I'm not saying anything because it just feels like Naomi doesn't want me to." It sounded even feebler out loud than she thought it would.

"But what I don't get is why you're not telling the police. It might actually help find her." He shook his head in disbelief. "No wonder you're having panic attacks."

"How dare you!" Bex heard the words pass her lips before she realized she was going to say them. "You don't know me. You don't know my sister. You don't know what it's like being either of us."

"No. You're right. I don't know you. I'm just the guy who thought you looked like you could do with somebody to talk to. Maybe I got that wrong." He stuck his hands in his pockets, took a step back and she could feel him slipping away. He'd been so nice – nicer than any of her real friends, for a start: had any of them offered to come and be with her? No. But Josh, a total stranger, had wanted to listen. He hadn't judged Naomi like Kay had, either.

"Josh." He scowled at her, waiting. "I know it sounds stupid. But I can't tell anyone about this. Not until I figure out what's going on with Naomi."

Because she's my twin, she added in her own head.

He blew out a long, slow breath and looked everywhere but at her. When his eyes finally met hers, he looked straight into them.

"You told *me*," he said.

"I guess so."

Bex poked at the button for the lights. There was something she was missing – like something she had dreamed. Like she had woken up after a deep night's sleep and could still feel her dreams lodged under her skin.

Blue, she thought.

14

Bex

"Uh, yeah, hello? Is this Bex?"

Bex hadn't recognized the number when she fumbled the phone out of her pocket but she answered it immediately. It could be...

But it wasn't Naomi.

"Who is this?"

"I saw your message. On your sister's page, yeah?"

"You know where Naomi is?"

She shot a meaningful glance at Josh. He took a step closer.

There was a long silence on the other end of the phone, then a sniff. "No. Yeah. I dunno." Another sniff.

"Do you know where she is?" Another pause. "Look, if you don't want to talk to me, why did you bother calling?"

"I dunno where she is, all right? All I know is that she was at this party last night..."

"With you?"

"Not exactly. We crashed it."

"Where was it?"

"I'm not telling you that!" He muttered something that might have been a swear word. Bex couldn't tell for sure.

"Then I'm going to the police."

A sigh. "There was some guy she was talking to."

A ball of ice formed in Bex's throat and dropped to the base of her stomach.

"A guy? What guy?"

"A guy in some band or something."

"Did she leave with him?"

"Maybe. I went upstairs with this girl, yeah –" he stopped, cleared his throat – "and when I came down, she'd gone."

"What band was it?"

"I dunno, do I? Overheard something about a backstage pass. Tell you what, though, if he was offering her a pass, that's where she is."

"That's *it*? You didn't care that she'd gone?"

"I'm not her dad, am I? I thought she was…"

"Stop." Bex couldn't bear to hear any more. "Do you know anything else? *Anything?*"

"That's it. I hope she turns up OK. She's all right, Naomi." It sounded like he was about to hang up.

"Wait!" Bex almost shouted down the phone. "What's your name? Please?"

He mumbled a word down the phone. "Sorry – what?"

"Dan."

And there was a click as the connection went dead.

Somewhere in the back of Bex's head, an idea flickered into life.

"I need to check Naomi's computer again," she said, more to herself than to Josh.

When she'd first heard Dan's voice an image had filled Bex's mind. Of being in a car ... a taxi. Music playing on the radio. A flash of a digital clock, 2.42 a.m. And that voice. Friendly. Familiar.

Bex had never met Dan but she could picture him. No, more than that. She could *see* him. Whoever Dan was, Bex was sure she'd find him on Naomi's Facebook page.

And what if I know what he looks like?

The mental image had been so clear. It wasn't just something she imagined: there was something too real about it. Like a memory – just one that belonged to someone else...

Playing hide-and-seek on a rainy afternoon. Squeezing behind the sofa, quiet as a mouse – barely even daring to breathe... And looking up to see Naomi beaming down from above.

"*How did you find me?*"

She'd forgotten that.

It was just a game, Naomi. Trying to pretend we were something special...

"That call – was it a lead?"

Bex bit her lip. "That guy, Dan, was with her last night at a party. He said someone from a band offered her a guest pass to a gig or something."

"But that's great, right?"

She raised an eyebrow at him and he shook his head. "I mean, it's one piece of the puzzle, isn't it? You know where she was last night, so now you just figure out where she went from there. What band?"

"He didn't know."

"So we need to find the band..."

"*How?*"

"I dunno." Josh kicked at a stone on the pavement. "My mate Nate would be good at this. He's seriously into music – he hasn't stopped wanging on about this festival he's going to this weekend."

"Festival?" she asked.

Josh nodded. "Yeah. He's been talking about it for months. Hemisphere?"

Hemisphere...

Oh. My. God. That's huge! Congratulations!

Why don't you come with us...?

The world danced in front of her eyes.

Blue.

"Hemisphere."

"Bex? You've gone all pale. You're not having another panic attack, are you?"

"No. No, I'm fine. Listen – your friend. Is he there already?"

Josh looked at his watch. "Should be."

"So the festival's already started?"

"Yeah, today – the campsite's been open since yesterday morning." He looked distracted. "Look, I know it's not really any of my business but can I make a suggestion?"

"Fire away."

"Tell the police about this guy, about all the tickets. You can't do this by yourself, Bex – it's too big."

"I told you, I can't."

"But they just want her home – isn't that what you want?"

"Yes, but…" She watched him watching her, trying to explain that she felt somehow responsible – for not knowing, not seeing, not being someone her sister could share her secrets with. Responsible for bringing Naomi home. Eventually, she sighed. "It's a twin thing. Please?" she added.

"A twin thing? Seriously?" He raised an eyebrow at her.

"You know, the whole identical twin thing."

"*Identical*," he muttered. "You didn't mention that."

The smell of hot dogs wafted past, a snatch of music carried through the air and disappeared.

At home, Bex's parents barely noticed Josh. They were happy enough to accept her mumbled explanation that he was a friend she'd bumped into earlier (mostly true) who had walked her home.

Naomi was at Hemisphere. Bex had no idea how, but as soon as Josh had said the word, she simply *knew*. Suddenly, she understood everything that had happened as clearly as if it had happened to her: the sneaking out, the party, the band, the festival. It made perfect sense.

What didn't make sense was *why.*

Was it her fault, or was Naomi playing a new version of hide-and-seek?

It was never a game.

Josh was leaning against the banister in the hallway, and Bex felt a rush of something between relief and gratitude. "I should go," he said.

Bex nodded. But at the same time, she wanted him to stay. "Thanks," she said after a minute. "For everything. And maybe…" She swallowed awkwardly. "Maybe we can meet up again sometime? When things are … normal? I can buy you a coffee to say thanks."

"I'd like that," he said.

Suddenly bright lights swirled in front of her eyes and she felt dizzy. She threw out a hand to balance herself but the feeling passed as quickly as it had appeared.

Josh didn't seem to noticed. "You don't need to thank me, though. I've not exactly done anything special." He tapped the carved wooden ball at the end of the banister with the palm of his hand. It fell off, bouncing along the floor. "Oops."

"Don't worry about it," Bex laughed, leaning over to scoop it up.

Naomi, sliding down the banister. Crashing into the ball at the end. It rolled along the floor, into the kitchen.

"Naomi! What on earth are you doing?"

"It wasn't me! It was Bex! Bex did it!"

The feeling of the wood underneath her, the rush of air whizzing through her hair as she sped along it…

Maybe it had been her after all.

She was still holding it as she closed the door behind him. Frowning, she set the ball back on its little wooden peg at the end of the banister and stared at it. She pulled out her phone and tried Naomi one more time, willing her to pick up … but it was just the same old voicemail. Didn't Naomi realize how worried everyone was?

"Doesn't she know? Can't she feel it, like we… Oh. OH."

Like we used to.

Bex froze halfway to the stairs, her phone gripped in her hand.

It was never a game.

The sounds. The swirling colours and lights. The smells. The flashes of memory that weren't – couldn't be – hers.

It's not possible. It was just a game.

Bex pushed the kitchen door open so hard that the handle banged back against the wall, making both her parents jump.

"Sorry. Sorry," she muttered. "It's just…"

They both looked at her expectantly.

"Before. When we were little." She ground to a halt. There was no way to say it without sounding stupid. She tried again. "Did we … have, like, a game we played? Me and Naomi."

"What do you mean, sweetheart?" Her mother asked.

"Like a secret, special game or something?"

"She means Naomi's mind-reading game." Bex's dad looked at her. "It was something the two of you used to do."

"Mind-reading game?" Bex tried very hard to keep her voice level.

"Naomi used to say the two of you were linked. She would pretend that she could hear what you were thinking, see and hear what you could. And, of course, you played up to it. Why do you ask?"

"Oh. Nothing. It was … something I remembered. That's all." Bex stepped out into the hall. Her heart pounding and her head full, she ran up the stairs.

Back in Naomi's room, she surveyed the chaos. She felt

like she was being handed a key; a key that would unlock everything … if only she knew where to find the door. Shards of her twin caught the light like a shattered mirror and glittered across the room – one here, one there. If she could piece the right ones together in the right way, she could solve the puzzle that Naomi had become. Sliding down to the floor, she pulled out Naomi's laptop and opened it up again.

"Right. Let's see what you've got for me." Beside her, her phone beeped with a message from Josh.

Hope everything OK. Keep me posted if there's any news. Speak to you tomorrow? J

There was a pause … and then a second message.

Wish we'd met some other way … but still glad we did.

Despite everything, it made her smile.

Naomi's secret Facebook feed hadn't changed much since the last time she'd looked at it. Someone had uploaded a couple of pictures from a festival and Bex's heart leaped … until she realized the festival was actually in Croatia. Even so, she found herself scanning the photos just in case. She scrolled back through the feed, looking for more pictures; anything – and then she stopped.

A photo had been uploaded that morning. There, in the background, was Naomi. All Bex could see was her arms and the very front of her face: the curl of her smile, her chin, her nose. An eye. It was definitely her.

Who was she talking to? The angle of the picture made it hard to see … there was a woman with her back to the camera, blocking her view. Naomi was talking to someone: Dan had said something about a band.

Hemisphere.

If Naomi was with a band, the festival staff would be able to get hold of them … and Naomi.

It would all be OK.

She opened another browser tab, typed the name of the festival into the search bar. She clicked on the festival website, scrolling down through the page in search of a contact. Everything about it felt right – even the logo looked familiar.

She knew it because Naomi knew it.

There. Right at the bottom: a phone number.

Heart beating so fast and hard she could feel it in her chest, she dialled the number.

It rang and rang and rang – and then an answering service kicked in with a recorded message.

Thank you for calling the Hemisphere festival office. We're sorry, but your call can't be answered at the moment as our staff are busy on site. Please leave a message or if you know the mobile number of the staff member you need to speak to, call direct.

Bex slammed her phone down on the floor. "What's the point of all these phones when nobody answers?" she shouted.

Opening her own email, she found a new message from Simeon waiting for her. It was exactly what she might have expected. He was vague, distant – and obviously thought that this was Naomi's way of getting his attention.

"What a dick." Bex sighed and deleted the message.

She lost track of time, sitting on the floor. The phone rang once or twice and every time her heart leaped … but when it became obvious that it wasn't Naomi, it sank again. Some time around eight o'clock her mum called up to her to come and eat something, but when she went into the kitchen, the spaghetti she tried to choke down felt and tasted like old cardboard. She pushed the rest of the bowl away. Her parents were worried now; really worried.

Back upstairs, Bex looked up at the first stars shining through the skylight.

"How can I help you if you won't let me?" Bex asked the silence, then – more out of habit than hope – she called her friends.

Ralph's phone went straight to voicemail, but Kay answered on the third ring.

"Hiiiiiiiii!" There was so much background noise, Bex could barely hear her. "Are you coming down or what? You'll never guess what Sarah and…"

"We still haven't found her."

"You're kidding? I thought you were calling… Hang on."

There was muffled crackling down the phone and the background noise suddenly dropped out.

"OK. I'm in the bathroom. What's happening?"

"I don't know. There's nothing."

Bex took a deep breath. It was Kay, after all…

"She left a note, but…"

"She what? What did it say?"

"It said she was fine, that was pretty much it."

"You are *shitting* me?" Kay's tone changed immediately. "Well, that's the Naomi we all know and love, then, isn't it? Selfish cow."

"Kay!" Her friend had never sounded so mean before.

"I'm sorry, but it's true. You're supposed to be celebrating! She's being selfish and you know it."

Bex bit her lip. Why didn't Kay understand?

"Look, I'm going to go… I just wanted you to know. And don't talk to anyone about this. Please?"

"Bex, I don't know what's going on…"

"Please. She's my sister, OK? Don't. Not even Ralph."

"Are you sure?"

"I'm sure. Have fun at the party and don't fall in the pool."

"Oh, Ralph already did that. And when I say 'fell', I actually mean 'was thrown'. It's a whole thing."

"Talk to you tomorrow." Bex lay back on her bed, shut her eyes and fell into the darkness.

15

Bex

Aged eleven

"Umm – do you know where…" Bex turns the printed map of the school round, "room seven is?"

She recognizes the girl in the corridor from registration earlier on, which means she's probably just as lost as they are. Behind her, Naomi scuffs her brand-new school shoes against the wall.

"Room seven!" The girl smiles broadly at Bex. "I can't find it, either."

"Should we go to the office and ask?"

"And admit that we're completely lost on our first day? I don't think so." She flicks her hair back over her shoulder and Bex feels a flash of envy. She's so confident.

Realizing there's someone behind Bex, the girl from their year peers around her … and freezes. Bex hears Naomi sigh: just like in primary school, they've been put in different registration forms here to limit exactly this kind of reaction. However, if the past few years have taught them anything, it's that separating them just makes it harder in the end. Besides, they still have classes together, so what's the point of that?

The girl from their year is now openly staring at them.

"You two! You're the twins, right? I heard about you! Rebecca and ... what was your name again?"

"Naomi."

"And it's Bex – not Rebecca. I'm Bex."

"Bex. That's such a cool name!"

Everything this girl says comes with an exclamation mark and Bex can already feel Naomi rolling her eyes.

"I'm Kay!"

"Hi, Kay." They both say it together; Bex doesn't mean for them to, but it happens anyway. Their voices together sound ... creepy.

"You did that on purpose."

"Did what?"

"Naomi..."

Silence.

Kay's eyes skip from face to face, looking for differences.

Bex saves her the trouble. "My hair's longer – well, it usually is." She tugs at her hair to demonstrate. "Umm. What else? I've got green studs in my ears, Naomi's got blue ones. Today, anyway. And I have a scar above my left eye. Naomi doesn't."

"Sorry?"

"You're trying to figure out how to tell which of us is which – it's OK," Bex laughs, "everybody does it.

118

It's fine." She brandishes the map again. "So. Room seven."

Kay ignores it. "What's it like being an identical twin?"

Bex throws Naomi a quick glance. "Complicated," she says – and waits for Naomi's sarcastic response. It never comes and when she glances back again, her twin is engrossed in the school club noticeboard.

"What?" Naomi asks in a prickly tone.

"Nothing," says Bex.

Kay slips her arm through Bex's and falls into step with her ... leaving Naomi three paces behind.

16

Naomi

The security office, when Naomi got there, was deserted; a laminated BACK IN FIVE MINUTES sign taped to the door. Naomi rattled the door handle and peered through the window for good measure, but it was very definitely empty.

"Well, that's just typical." She leaned against the wall and pondered her options. Without her wallet, she only had the cash in her pocket – which, after a quick count, came to thirty-seven pounds and forty-three pence – to last the whole festival and the journey home. Without her phone... Well, people had managed without them in the old days, hadn't they? It would be an adventure. The mental picture of her parents flashed through her mind again but she pushed it away. She wasn't going to start thinking like that now. She'd left them a note, hadn't she? And it was only for a couple of days...

Then there was the problem of the stolen backstage lanyard. It was the lanyard that had made her decide to go to the security office after all – without her pass, she couldn't get back to the band or the van – and she was fairly sure she wasn't going to be able to blag her way through. She needed a new pass. And the only way she was going to be able to get one of those was to somehow get hold of Ethan or Ollie.

There was no way she could speak to them before their set – she'd just have to wait until they'd finished and, in the meantime, hadn't she come to the festival to enjoy it?

Untying Max's blue hoodie from around her waist, she slipped it over her shoulders. It smelled like orange juice and metal and a man she didn't know, but it was warm.

Abandoning the empty office, she headed for the stalls at the side of the main arena, away from the stages. There were hundreds of them, laid out in neat rows like streets. Some of the stalls were funny little wooden chalets with roofs and windows, while others were barely more than a couple of planks on trestles. There were places selling T-shirts and dresses, flower crowns and wigs (which made Naomi touch her own wig, now firmly pinned over her hair), flags, inflatable chairs and dreamcatchers. The last stall in the row sold old-style disposable cameras, the ones made of plastic and cardboard. Who would bother with using one of those and getting the photos developed when they had their phones with them?

She looked at the camera stall again and the bored-looking guy in charge of it. Naomi waved at him and handed over six pounds fifty for a camera. She'd just have to be careful how much she spent on food and drink. Leaning against the corner of the stall, she took a photo of the colourful dreamcatchers at the stall next door, and then another one: this time of two girls with feathers plaited into their hair.

Why hadn't she thought about photography before? Maybe she should have...

For a while, she wandered up and down the lines of stalls, trying to find interesting angles or flashes of unexpected colour. It was the kind of thing Bex would be good at: she had an artist's eye for the world. Naomi had never been able to do that – but where Bex saw the world, Naomi saw people.

She turned a corner into a lane of stalls dedicated to incense and e-cigarettes, and then she rounded another corner and the air changed – filling with the scents of a dozen different foods. Burgers, hot dogs, falafel, fish curries, spiced soup; things roasting, grilling, baking. Tucking the camera into the pocket of the hoodie, she joined the jostle in search of food – in all the chaos of unloading the van and losing her bag, she hadn't managed to get anything to eat yet.

Her stomach growled at the thought, making her clamp her hand across her midriff in case anyone heard. When *had* she last eaten? She couldn't think of anything since the toast she'd had last night, right before Dan had called. She didn't know what time it was – mid-afternoon by now, definitely, but all her body cared about was that it was time to eat. Everything smelled so good, too… She strolled up and down, checking the prices and looking at the food, and eventually settled for some kind of flatbread filled with vegetables and non-specific meat. It was the cheapest and the guy behind the counter looked like Chris Hemsworth, so that was that. It tasted OK, although she tried not to think about why the meat wasn't actually named.

Grabbing a bottle of water as she went, Naomi ducked out of the flow of the crowd and headed for the slope she passed earlier. One of the smallest stages had already started up and seemed to be occupied by a trio playing northern soul standards … on sitars. She kept walking until she reached the bank, climbing it until she found a reasonable space. From her spot halfway up, she could see most of the way across the field to the main stage.

But the more she looked around, the more she saw that everyone around her was *with* somebody. In fact, the only other people she had seen on their own were a drunk guy passed out on the grass, and Max – and Max definitely gave off an air of being OK on his own.

She took another bite of the flatbread, shrugging off the thought, but suddenly the meat felt greasy and she wished there was someone she could joke about it to. She wished Bex was there. She forced the mouthful down and tried to ignore the whispering in her left ear. It was probably just feedback from the speakers.

There were so many people there ... she didn't know any of them. And none of them knew her.

And if none of them knew her, what was the point of pretending? She could just be ... Naomi.

Naomi who was miles from home with no phone and no plan, and – despite being surrounded by people – completely alone. And who wasn't sure she liked it.

No, she thought. *I just need to not be sitting here eating shitty food. I can still get it sorted out, get backstage again in a bit. It'll be fine. Get a grip.*

She stood up, brushing the flour from her hands – and then she saw her. At the bottom of the slope.

"Bex?"

A couple of people turned to look at Naomi ... but not the figure with her back to her.

She took a step forwards. How could Bex be there? How had she found her?

A guy carrying a huge flag over his shoulder walked between them and stopped, pulling out his phone to take a photo of the stage ... and by the time Naomi dodged around him, the figure had vanished.

Naomi.

Her name was as clear as if Bex had whispered it straight into her ear – but her sister wasn't there.

Although that didn't mean she hadn't heard it.

The hairs on the back of Naomi's neck stood up and she felt a prickle running down her spine. In an instant she understood what it meant: she was as sure of it as she had ever been, as sure as she always used to be that she could draw back *this* curtain or look under *that* bed and find her sister looking right back at her.

Bex had remembered.

She actually remembered – at last. She remembered how they used to be.

And just as quickly as she realized it, she felt the anger building. Anger for all those times she had wished Bex would remember and she didn't; for all the times her sister had shut her out.

"No, Naomi. We have to keep it a secret. It'll be more fun that way."

"No, Naomi. We have to keep it a secret. People will think it's weird."

"No, Naomi. We have to keep it a secret. People will think you're nuts."

"No, Naomi. Are you kidding? I have no idea what you're talking about."

All those times … and suddenly, Bex remembered?

No, thought Naomi bitterly. *Too little, too late.*

By the time she calmed down again, more of the stages were starting to open and music could be heard drifting across the site. Naomi's stomach churned as she brushed the grass from her clothes and joined the throngs of people heading for the stages. She picked her way towards the stage where she knew Parrish were playing. They'd just started and maybe she was in a bad position, but the music didn't exactly sound … good.

She found a spot further into the field and folded herself into a sitting position to listen. It was the least she could do, she thought. In front of her, a guy with a mohican was waving an enormous banner back and forth, completely blocking her view of the stage. The screens on either side of the stage displayed a striking array of pixels.

There was a massive howl of feedback and – as one – the crowd around her groaned. The band's set limped on and a girl with long, plaited red hair, sitting on the edge of a nearby group glanced over at Naomi, smiling.

"They're not great, are they? I like your hair, by the way," she said.

"Thanks. And these guys? Unfortunately, I know them so I've got to report back on how they sounded. I might lie."

The girl flushed with embarrassment. "Are they your

friends? I'm so sorry!"

"Sorry they're my friends, or sorry for saying they're shit?" Naomi shot back – but the girl looked so upset that she immediately felt bad. "I'm kidding. I don't know them all that well – and you're right. They're really not great."

"How do you know them?" The redheaded girl shuffled round in her spot, opening up a space for Naomi. "I'm Siena."

"Naomi. I met them at a party. Friends of friends, you know?" she tried to make it sound casual.

"So how come you're slumming it out here? I'd have thought you'd be backstage!" Siena laughed.

Naomi gave a careless sort of shrug. "The sound's not so good backstage."

"It's not so good front of stage," sniggered one of the boys in the group, obviously listening in on their conversation. He offered Naomi a plastic bottle. "You want some cider?"

"Is *that* what that is?" Naomi arched an eyebrow at it and was pleased to see them grin. She shook her head. Her stomach didn't feel right after eating the Mystery Meat and flushing it out with a load of flat, warm, sweet cider wasn't going to do it much good.

They sat in a companionable sort of silence, watching and listening, until with an almighty crash of cymbals and a howl of guitar, the band's set ended. The applause was ... subdued. Naomi doubted Ethan would notice anyway. She stood up, hopping from one foot to another to get the feeling back into her toes. If she wanted to get backstage again, she'd have to catch them as they came off.

"Well, I guess I better head off..."

There was some shuffling in the group.

"Are you sure?" Siena actually sounded disappointed. "You're welcome to stay and hang out with us if you like?"

"Thanks, but no. I should really go – maybe tell the guys they were good." She wrinkled her nose for comic effect. "Or something, anyway."

"If you change your mind. We're going to be here until at least..." Siena pulled a crumpled piece of paper covered in scrawled handwriting from her pocket. "Until after Fallstars."

"Maybe I'll catch up with you later. It was nice meeting you..." she added.

"You, too, Naomi," Siena said.

It was only as she walked away that Naomi realized Siena might actually have meant it.

17

Bex

Aged seven

"Will you two stop dawdling? We're late enough as it is!"

But Bex doesn't want to rush along the high street and nor does Naomi. It's almost Christmas and the lights strung across the street are so pretty against the sky. Even though it's only four o'clock, it's almost dark and everything sparkles. The windows of the local shops have all got tinsel and fairy lights twinkling on and off, on and off. Bex wishes it would stay this way all year round.

"I've got a stone in my shoe!" Naomi yelps, stopping so suddenly that Bex almost crashes into her. She watches as her twin yanks off her trainer, leaning against the estate agent's window, and turns her shoe upside down. A very small stone tumbles out and bounces along the pavement. Naomi peers at it, then looks offended.

"It felt *much* bigger than that."

Bex wriggles her toes inside her boots.

Nothing.

"Rebecca! Naomi! Come on!"

Their mother is standing in the entrance of the

hairdressing salon, holding the door open.

The hairdresser waves them over to the battered little sofa in the waiting area of the salon. As Bex drops into her seat, Naomi makes a beeline for the bowl of chocolates on the table. Bex, for once, reaches past them. Instead, she picks up one of the battered hairstyle catalogues that sit on the shelf under the table.

They've both worn their hair exactly the same ever since Bex can remember. Maybe this time she could ask for something different. Sometimes, Bex thinks, it would be good not to have to share *everything*.

Last week in Assembly, one of the Year Six girls – Ruth – had come in with a new hairstyle. Her waist-long plait had been cropped into a neat bob ... and she looked amazing. Bex had thought she could easily pass for a Year Seven. She looked so *mature*, and as soon as their mum told them she was taking them to get their hair cut, Bex knew what she wanted. Sitting on the old familiar sofa, she checked page after page of the hairdresser's look-book, trying to find what she wanted.

She's concentrating so hard that she doesn't even hear the hairdresser come back and ask which of them is going first. Naomi looks at her: she hates getting her hair cut, so Bex *always* goes first. But this time, Naomi goes first.

Bex keeps on flipping through the hairstyles. She's found one that's almost perfect, but it has a fringe.

Her hair doesn't have to be exactly like the picture…

Naomi is in the chair longer than usual. Much longer. And when Bex glances up, she sees the piles of hair on the floor. Her eyes follow the back of the chair, up to where the hairdresser is running a comb through Naomi's hair.

What's left of it.

Naomi's hair has been cut into a perfect bob.

18

Naomi

"Sorry, love. No one's coming in or out for a while. Backstage is being cleared until Mr Laing and his entourage have left. He's requested a sterile area."

"A sterile area?" Naomi wrapped her fingers through the wire of the fence as though she could somehow pull herself through it, on to the other side where the security guard stood, shaking his head. When she'd tried the security office again, it had been open – but the staff there had kept her waiting for ages, then shrugged and sent her back to the fence she'd come through earlier. It didn't matter how many times she'd tried to explain the problem to them, they shook their heads: she didn't have the paperwork for a lanyard, so they couldn't replace it. Sorry, but rules are rules…

"It means, darlin', that it doesn't matter if you own the field – if you're not in a band or with a band, you're not coming through."

"But I *am* with a band! Parrish. They played earlier and I need to see them – that's what I'm trying to tell you.

I lost my lanyard."

"Of course you did."

"No, I really did."

Just as she was about to go through the whole saga again, she spotted a familiar figure making their way along the walkway from the stages.

Ethan.

"Hey! Ethan!" She waved. "Over here!"

Hearing his name, Ethan stopped and frowned. The security guard half turned to watch what he did – which meant, to Naomi's horror, he had a clear view of Ethan spotting her through the fence … then narrowing his eyes and shrugging. "Never seen her before," he called to the security guard, who turned round again and gave Naomi a stern glare.

"He's just trying to mess with me," she said, but the guard folded his arms.

Without another word of protest, she turned and walked back across the main field, all the way to the hill where she'd been sitting earlier … where she retched and threw up what was left of the Mystery Meat.

Legs wobbling, Naomi sat down before she fell down. "Shit," she muttered, wiping her mouth with the back of her hand. "Shit, shit, shit, shit, shit."

Bright colours swirled in front of her eyes. They stayed there even when she closed them.

Freckles.

Freckles and a checked shirt.

Naomi raised her hands to her face; touched her cheeks. They felt hot.

Who did she know with freckles?

Breathing deeply, she sat there with her eyes closed, waiting for the nausea to pass. She tried to listen to the voices around her, the music drifting over from the stages…

Bex, sliding down the banister. Crashing into the ball at the end. It rolled along the floor, into the kitchen.

The feeling of the wood underneath her, the rush of air whizzing through her hair as she sped along it…

Had it been Bex? Or had it been her? She couldn't remember. There were so many memories that overlapped. In Naomi's head, they'd belonged to them both – or at least, that was how it used to feel…

Freckles.

Freckles and a checked shirt.

Words on a screen: Wish we'd met some other way … but still glad we did.

Not. Her. Memory.

The link. The Bex-and-Naomi, Naomi-and-Bex. Their secret. The connection they'd always had; the one she thought had gone forever…

It was back.

This didn't feel like an old memory. This was new.

"Wish we'd met…" she whispered to herself. What was wrong with the way they'd met? Unless it wasn't *how*, so much as *when*? Like … today?

This was *today*.

Checked shirt and freckles was someone Bex had met *today*.

"No," she said – loudly enough that a guy with dreadlocks piled on top of his head turned to stare at her. She shoved the thought of her sister away; if Bex had actually been there – standing in front of her – she would have pushed her away, too.

"No, no, no. You don't get to do this. Not now. No."

How many times had she wished that the connection between them would open again? How many times had she been desperate to know what Bex was thinking, how she was feeling … to feel a little less alone in her own head?

Naomi wrapped her arms around herself and forced her legs to start moving. Halfway up the hill, she turned to look over the site spread out in front of her. The lights of the main stage blazed brightly against a sky already shot through with the pinks and purples of early evening. The screens of phones held aloft were tiny blue-white sparks. There was shouting, music, noise.

Even though she fought it, she couldn't stop herself

135

from thinking about her sister. Bex would never have got herself into this mess. Bex's idea of a wild night was messaging her friends, wondering whether she should have olives on her pizza.

But that wasn't what Naomi wanted.

No, she thought, shaking her head. *I'm here for a reason.*

She'd thought she could interview bands backstage... Well, that hadn't worked out, but there was still the camera. She felt in her pocket for the disposable camera.

It was gone.

She thought back to the office ... sitting on the narrow bench while she waited... She'd taken it out then, snapped a...

She'd put it on the bench beside her. And forgotten about it.

"SHIT!" This time she screamed it, and for a second she almost imagined she could hear her voice echoing across the festival.

At the very top of the hill was a ring of standing stones surrounded by a ring of streaming banners in all the colours of the rainbow. In the middle of the circle, a group of people appeared to be doing yoga. Beyond the stones, the hill flattened – and in one direction, a hazy white glow came from the temporary floodlights at the entrance to the big camping field. In the other ... a pair of flaming torches as high as her shoulders marked the beginning of a pathway ... to where?

Slipping past the yoga-types, she ducked around another group heading from the campsite, as one of them shouted, "Nate! Over here!" The guy turned and whooped, posing for a photo. She peered down the side of the hill. The torches were the start of a path, curling down and around the back of the hill. There was music, too – but it wasn't the bands and the thumping bass of the main site. It was drums, played with fingertips and palms; a sound like a pipe, a whistle, carried by the wind. And while there were still people on the path, there weren't many – just a handful wandering up or down. It was quieter. Exactly what she needed.

At the end of the torchlit path was another cluster of tents and stalls but here everything was lit with strings of glowing lanterns and the smell of burgers was replaced by something like lavender. A woman was sitting beside a brazier, her legs crossed as a man in white kneeled behind her and rubbed his fingers through her hair. A blackboard in front of them read: 'Scalp massage: release your stress and drift away!' A sign opposite advertised reflexology; another suggested she consider 'chakra realignment'. Slowly she walked between the stalls and breathed in the scent of herbs.

"You OK there, my lovely?" asked a woman from a tarot stall. She smiled at Naomi.

"Fine. I'm fine."

"Ever had your cards read?"

"No, no thanks. Not my kind of thing."

Ahead of her, a young couple were walking along, looking at the stalls. They walked with their arms round each other's shoulders and with a sudden pang she remembered Simeon.

That could have been him and me.

Except Simeon had turned out to be a tosser.

Pictures tumbled past her eyes – things she knew she hadn't seen...

Cake crumbs.

A photo of the two of them, the edges soft.

The photo from under her pillow – but this wasn't her memory.

Naomi could feel her sister there, like someone standing on the other side of a door, waiting for it to be opened. Like their connection had never been broken.

But it had. And it had been Bex who shut the door. She'd done it once: what if she did it again?

It hurt too much.

"You feel so alone, don't you? I can sense it from here," said a voice – another stallholder that Naomi hadn't even noticed. She was a short woman with spiky silver-grey hair and bright black eyes that reminded her of beetles. "You don't think anyone can understand, but I do.

I've seen it before – more times than you'd imagine."

"What?"

"It hurts. When you're bound to someone you don't want to be bound to, it feels like they're an anchor, weighing you down. Holding you back." She leaned closer. "It's in your aura."

"Right." Naomi took a careful step back but the woman leaned in even closer.

"I can take it away. The pain."

"You … what?"

"I can take it away."

"No. Thanks. Really. It's just my sister."

"A twin?" The woman tipped her head to one side. Naomi didn't like the way she was looking at her.

"How…?"

"People don't understand what it's like – people without, I mean. They can't know what it's like to have that connection, whether you want it or not. To be a part of another mind and soul, and to have another person be a part of you."

"No. No, they don't. No one does." And because they didn't know, they couldn't understand how much it hurt to lose it. She'd gone through that once – to go through it again… Naomi was sure it wouldn't just hurt her. It would *break* her. She couldn't do it another time.

"You'll never have to worry about being hurt like that."

The beetle-eyed woman smiled again. "I can free you. I can help you break that connection. For good."

Naomi took another step back, suddenly wanting to be anywhere but here … and trod on a battered Converse trainer – and the foot inside it.

"Ouch!" said the guy. He was one half of the couple she'd been watching. He was the same height as her, with dark hair that fell half across his face.

"Sorry," she muttered – but he was looking past her and reading the sign outside the woman's tent.

"Psychic healer," he whispered. "You are stronger than you believe! Your mind can help you heal! Trust me to guide you through…" He made a snorting sound. "Well, that's bullshit. You want to be careful messing with your head. It's a lot darker in there than you'd think."

"In my head?" Naomi asked.

As he shook his head, she saw the long scar running down one side of his face. "In anybody's head. Problem is, once you let it out … how do you put it back in?"

"Oi! Grey! Come on – we're going to miss…" His girlfriend ran over. She stopped by his side; wound her fingers through his.

"Sorry, Iz." He lifted her hand to his lips and planted a loud, wet-sounding kiss on her knuckles.

"You're disgusting," she laughed as they turned away.

Naomi turned his words over in her mind. Maybe it was

dark inside her head, but she didn't care. Dark and quiet – that didn't sound so bad.

"You'd rather be lonely alone. That's it, isn't it?"

The healer ... psychic ... whoever she was, was still there.

If Naomi was going to feel so lonely, she might as well *be* alone.

"How much?" Naomi asked, her fingers closing on the last of the cash in her pocket.

"How much do you have?"

"I've only got this…" Naomi held out her open palm with the money she had left on it.

"Then it'll cost everything you have."

The woman closed her fist around Naomi's and when she took her hand away, the money was gone.

The area behind the stall was hidden by a thick curtain. Beyond it was a small, rickety stool sitting in the middle of an old carpet. The whole place smelled damp and mouldy. "Take a seat, we'll begin in a moment…"

The woman pulled a bundle of leaves from a pocket and held them over a disposable plastic lighter. The flame caught and thick scented smoke curled up. "Sage and lavender. To clear your mind."

"Mmm." Naomi's head spun as the smoke thickened.

"Here. You need to drink this." A small, chipped teacup appeared under her nose. It had faded roses painted on it, and a collection of dried leaves and bits of twig floating in yellow-green water. It smelled awful.

"What is it?"

"Herbal tea."

"What kind?"

"My own."

The smoke wafted around her again.

Naomi shook her head. "I'm not drinking that."

"Suit yourself. But I can't help you if you don't."

Naomi eyed the cup. "Will it take long?"

"That depends on you." The woman swished the burning twigs above Naomi's head. The smoke made her eyes water, and the smell of the tea even more so … but she tipped her head back and gulped it down in one mouthful.

"Some psychic links go deeper than others," the woman continued as Naomi gagged, clamping her hand over her mouth to stop herself from throwing up again. "But twins – and *identical* twins – that's a deeper bond than most."

"I never told you we were identical."

"I told you – I can feel it."

The cold was burning her up from the inside; it was a thousand knives sawing away at everything she was.

This was emptiness and loneliness.

"No." It was too quiet, and suddenly there was no air in her lungs… She had to say it again. Louder.

The woman was standing behind her, chanting under her breath.

"No. Stop." Naomi staggered to her feet, knocking the stool over.

"I'm sorry – what did you say?"

"I don't want it. I can't. I can't."

Everything was spinning and she wanted … needed … it to stop.

"Are you sure? I can't give you your money back…"

There was more, but Naomi didn't hear it. She was fighting to pull back the curtain, falling out into the fresh air and gulping it down.

She had to get away from the tent, from the smoke, from the woman.

Naomi tumbled out of the tent – and into the darkness.

19

Bex

It happened in the middle of the night.

Bex had been having uneasy dreams, chasing Naomi down never-ending corridors and through houses with too many rooms. In one, Naomi was on the other side of a locked door and Bex could hear her calling for help … but every time she found the right key, there was another door behind it. She was fighting her way up from sleep, not quite awake and not quite dreaming, when she smelled smoke.

I have to wake up, she thought. But when she tried to sit up, she couldn't.

As the smell grew stronger, Bex panicked. A horrible taste filled her mouth, like stagnant water and rotten wood … and then it started to hurt.

Everything hurt.

It was cold and hot all at once and everything was tipping; sliding sideways. A tearing sensation in her head, inside her. Something burning its way through every corner of her mind. Being pulled apart.

Naomi.

Something had been ripped away from her; something that she hadn't even realized was there until it left a hole behind. Wave after wave of nausea washed over her, and the cold and the emptiness dug deeper and deeper into her…

And as suddenly as it began, it stopped. It was gone.

Naomi.

Naomi had always been there, on the other side of a door. It was all real.

The memories that weren't quite hers; the ones where she couldn't tell whether they were hers or Naomi's. There really *was* a link between them. How could she have forgotten? Now it made sense: all of it – even this deep feeling that *she* had to find Naomi; why she had been so sure that only she could. It was because of *this*.

Shaking all the way to her fingertips, Bex tried to sit up.

What if she's…

She couldn't bring herself to think it, never mind say it. "No. That's not possible. It's just not."

Bex sagged back against her pillow, feeling like someone had reached into her chest and ripped out half her heart, leaving the threads that had held it together dangling.

Bex watched the dawn crawl across the ceiling of her room, the light turning it ever-paler shades of grey, then orange, then pink, and finally a buttery early morning shade of yellow. She hadn't been able to go back to sleep – her mind was too busy, and thoughts whirled past so fast she could barely catch them.

Naomi can't be dead.

I'd know. I'd know – wouldn't I?

Wouldn't I?

In the silence of her room, she cleared her mind and thought, loudly; making a silent call to the only person who could ever hear it.

Naomi.

But there was no answer.

And for the first time since she'd realized her sister wasn't in the exam room, Bex felt really afraid.

Something had happened but she *was* still alive. But the more certain she became that Naomi was alive, the more she thought about the other possibilities. And the one she kept coming back to was that Naomi had somehow abandoned her.

"Why?"

She got out of bed and tiptoed out of her room, pushed Naomi's door open and stepped inside.

She remembered. She remembered everything: whispering to Naomi late at night inside her head and

146

Naomi whispering back; how Naomi would always tell the punchlines to her jokes (and how angry it made her). How, when Naomi got chickenpox, Bex had itched all over even though there hadn't been a spot on her, and how, when Bex broke her ankle at primary school, it had been Naomi who limped for weeks. It was as if someone had punched a hole in the wall between them and memory after memory was pouring through.

She looked online, combing through articles about twins for anything that explained what she'd felt in the night, but nothing seemed to fit. But nobody else was twinned with Naomi, were they? How could it be the same? One thing was for sure, though: there was something between them. Maybe even between all identical twins. There were countless reports of pairs who claimed to be able to feel what the other was feeling; one in London, say, knowing when another was in an accident in Mumbai. Things that no one had quite been able to explain...

She heard her dad's footsteps on the landing. "Rebecca?" There was panic in his voice when he found her bedroom empty.

"In Naomi's room," she called back and, a moment later, the door opened.

"You OK?" he asked, peering in.

"OK as I can be," she said. "I didn't sleep very well."

She watched him take in the posters, the jewellery, the

skateboard and trainers and notebooks. The piles of clothes and the gymnastics ribbons. Even the small, threadbare teddy bear sitting on top of the chest of drawers.

"Mr Snuffles," he said quietly. "You remember him?"

"Didn't I have one, too?"

"You did. We bought him for Naomi one birthday when you were little – we got you a cat one – but you both wanted Mr Snuffles. In the end, we got so sick of you arguing over him that your mother bought another one, just the same. She called him 'Mr Snuffles the Second', but neither of you wanted him."

A memory flickered through Bex's mind: *Naomi screaming, "He's not the same! He's not! I hate him!"*

Their mother, holding Mr Snuffles the Second out to her.

"But he looks the same! See?"

"It doesn't matter! Just because he looks the same doesn't mean he is!"

Naomi had got permanent custody of Mr Snuffles, while Bex had had to accept Mr Snuffles the Second. She didn't even know where he was any more.

"I'd forgotten," she whispered.

He paused and it looked as though he might say something else, but he didn't, and the door clicked shut behind him.

Bex stared at Mr Snuffles. He had a bald patch on the inside of his ear and she knew exactly how it would feel if she rubbed it.

How could she know that, when Naomi had guarded him so jealously?

There was more to this. There had to be. And if she knew things like that – her sister's private, secret memories – then she could find her. All Bex needed was a couple more clues; a few extra dots she could connect that would lead to Naomi. She took a long look around the room, forcing her eyes to check everything they saw.

"OK then. Better get started."

There was nothing under the bed Bex hadn't already found. Nothing in the wardrobe. Nothing in the desk drawers. Nothing under the mattress and nothing under the chest of drawers. Nothing useful in its drawers, either. But the bottom drawer, when she slid it out, felt heavier than the others; it jammed as she opened it and made a scraping noise like it was too big for its slot in the chest.

Bex yanked the whole thing out on to the floor, flipping it upside down and tipping a tangle of jumpers across the carpet.

There.

Stuck to the bottom of the drawer was a notebook. Bex's hand hovered over it.

Do I even want to know?

If she read it – whatever it was – it would be a betrayal. Naomi had hidden the book.

But maybe it would help. Maybe it would show her what Naomi was going through. She wondered when she'd stopped just knowing – she used to *know*, didn't she? Had there been a day, a week, an afternoon?

It was a diary: the handwriting on the first couple of pages looked like it was Naomi's when they were ten or eleven. There were doodles and the occasional heart with a name in the middle (scribbled out). Bex stopped flipping at a page where Naomi had been practising a signature – for a completely different name. On the next page the name was drawn in a box surrounded by little lights. It was Naomi's acting phase. Bex smiled to herself. Her stage name.

She turned a couple more pages and the entries changed. There were fewer doodles and much more writing. The handwriting got neater, too – and then, after a dozen or so entries, the writing became a black scrawl with words underlined and crossed-through … and then stopped altogether.

Bex stared at the blank pages. "What the hell happened?"

She flipped back to the first neat entry. It was their first day at secondary school, almost exactly as she remembered it. As Bex flipped a page, she spotted a name with a ring around it, every time it turned up.

Kay.

Puzzled, she went back to the beginning. It was a couple

of days after they'd started school. Naomi felt that Kay was coming between them, pushing her out. That day, she had deliberately (as Naomi saw it) made sure there was only space for two of them to sit together at lunch. That didn't exactly sound like Kay to Bex, but...

The next entry, Kay had arranged something with Bex at the same time she was supposed to be doing something else with Naomi. Bex didn't remember that, either – and she was ashamed to read that she'd told Naomi they could do *their* thing any time.

She'd picked Kay over her twin? She didn't remember it being like that at all – Naomi had always been there with them at the start of school, until one day she hadn't. She'd just ... stopped. If anything, it was *Naomi* who pushed people away. She always had.

Hadn't she?

With a growing sense of unease, Bex read on.

Entry after entry went the same way: Kay, Kay, Kay...

And then it came to the last one.

I just like it better when it's the two of us. Without Naomi.

Kay had said that?

That wasn't possible. Kay would *never* say something like that...

Would she?

Like you said – sometimes, your sister's just a bit weird.

A conversation she'd had with Kay; joking about their

families – about Kay's brother, about Naomi. Had she said Naomi was weird? Maybe.

But she hadn't *meant* it. Not really. The full horror sank in: if Kay *had* said that to Naomi, then not only was Kay a different person, a different kind of friend to the one Bex had believed her to be, but Naomi would have had no way of knowing that she wasn't serious. She would have thought Bex meant it.

She had thought Bex meant it.

She still did.

It's my fault.

And what made it worse was that she hadn't even *noticed*. She had let Naomi slip away … and now it was too late.

"No," she said again, shaking her head. "It's not too late. I'm going to find you, Naomi. I'm going to fix this."

20

Bex

Bex's Facebook feed was crammed with photos from yesterday's party. One series of shots showed Ralph standing at the edge of the pool and then flying through the air towards the water. Several pictures had actually managed to catch him in mid-air but the final one was of him standing dripping wet and grinning in the water. She smiled: that was Ralph all over.

And then there were the messages. The post she'd put up about Naomi had spread and now there were dozens of notes from people at school – some of them nice, some of them … not so much. Feeling defensive and overwhelmed, she slammed her laptop shut.

"Bex? There's someone here to see you!"

Her dad's voice pulled her back to the house. Kay must have come round. How could she look Kay in the eye, knowing what her friend had done? Slowly, she walked downstairs. Perhaps she should start small; start with telling Kay about the random guy who had helped her and been so sweet…

And who was standing in the middle of her kitchen with a cardboard tray of takeaway coffees in one hand and a small paper bag in the other.

"Oh."

"Umm. Hi," said Josh sheepishly. "I wanted to see how you were – I hope you don't mind? I just thought ... if there was any news, or if there wasn't, you might need a coffee. And breakfast."

"Let me," her mum said, stepping forward and taking the bag Josh was holding out. "That's very kind of you, umm?" She looked at Bex.

"This is Ollie," she said. Who was *Ollie*? "Sorry. I mean Josh. Don't know where that came from..." She changed tack. "He walked me home yesterday – remember?"

"Oh yes. Yes," her mum said absently.

Bex raised an eyebrow at Josh and he shuffled his feet.

Her dad cleared his throat. "Why don't you go upstairs? We're expecting the family liaison officer."

Bex's face must have given away the bubbling mix of hope and panic she suddenly felt, because he shook his head. "No, there's no news. She's just ... checking in, I suppose..." He tailed off, staring at the floor.

Bex took two coffees from the tray and led Josh upstairs.

"Look, Bex, I don't mean to be in the way or anything. I get it if you want to be on your own. My dad sent me out to pick up Grandad's coat from the police station and

I just… I just thought…"

"It's fine, really." Bex passed him a coffee. "It's good you're here." She pulled out her desk chair for him to sit on, perching herself on the edge of her bed.

"It is?" He brightened, and flopped on to the chair. "So you haven't heard anything?"

Bex took a breath, about to answer – then paused. What should she say? "No, but … I don't know."

"You don't know?"

"It's complicated."

He was watching her intently.

She swallowed a mouthful of coffee. "Thank you, by the way. For this. It's really nice of you."

"You're welcome. I should have called first. Given you some warning. Sorry."

"Warning?" Bex didn't understand.

He looked pointedly at her and raised an eyebrow. "Nice pyjamas."

"What? I … oh." She looked down at herself. She hadn't even realized she was still wearing her pyjamas.

"Is that a cat playing a saxophone?"

"Yes. Yes, it is."

"Bold choice."

"I like to think so." She took a big swig of coffee to cover her embarrassment and choked on it. Her eyes watered as she forced it down.

155

There was an uncomfortable silence. Yesterday morning, all she'd been worried about was getting through one more maths paper, and after that it would be pizza and pyjamas all the way. She looked down at her pyjamas again.

Stupid pyjamas.

Josh took a swig of coffee. "So what's going on with the police?"

"Not much – not yet. If she doesn't contact us or the police by tomorrow morning, they can start circulating a missing person's notice. Train stations, airports, 'have you seen this girl?' pictures…" The thought made her throat close up. It wouldn't come to that. She wouldn't let it. She couldn't.

"You think it's your fault, don't you?" Josh shook his head. "Man. How can it be your fault? It's not like you shoved your sister out the door, is it?" He frowned. "Look, I don't have a twin or anything, so maybe I don't get it – but you're not responsible for somebody else's choices, Bex. She's not you and you're not her, and you're not supposed to be."

Bex rubbed her hands across her face.

He gave her a sad smile and continued. "So maybe I don't get that part. But here's the part I do get – you don't know what's going on with someone you care about and you're scared. I've been going with my dad to pick my grandad up from the police station for the last five years.

I've *seen* him. I've watched him go through the same thing over and over again. It's not the same but I understand, OK?" He tried to make his smile a little brighter but it didn't really work.

"I don't know. It's just ... sometimes I think I'm the only one who *sees* her. Does that make sense?"

"Look, I get it. You love your sister and you want to look out for her. You say you're the only one who knows who she really is and you act like she's betrayed you by not telling you everything – which I get – but ... don't you think you're just the same?"

Josh's words fell through the air like rocks.

"What?"

"You're not telling the truth, either, are you?"

Bex paused. "No. I'm not," she admitted.

That's up to Naomi. When I find her. And I can find her; I will find her.

"Have you got any brothers or sisters?" Bex asked.

"Nope. Just me. Although you could say Grandad's like having a kid in the family, you know?"

"Does he live with you?"

"He moved in a few years ago. Dad was worried he'd leave the gas on or something – and then, when he's bad…"

"Has he ever been gone for longer than an hour or two?"

"Once or twice. Just before he moved in, we lost him for

a whole weekend. Dad was out of his *mind*."

"But he was all right? He came back?"

"Turned out he'd got on a coach. Somehow nobody noticed and he made it all the way to Plymouth."

"No!" Bex covered her mouth with her hand. "What happened?"

"Nothing. He got off and just sat on a bench at the bus station. When we eventually tracked him down and Dad picked him up, apparently all he said was 'I knew you'd come'. It's crazy, because all the other times he's got really upset. That time, he was just … calm."

"Did he realize where he was?"

"I don't know. But there must have been something going on that stopped him getting wound up." He ran his hands through his hair. "Who knows how it all works up there, right? That's what Dionne, the family support officer, says. She's the one who usually has to calm him down when he gets to the station."

"Mmm." Bex pulled at the edge of the cardboard rim of her cup. It started to unroll under her fingers. "You think there was something going on in his head?"

"There's plenty going on in his head. I've seen him go from being … my grandad, you know? … to being the version of him he was before I was born, before my dad was born even. He doesn't know who I am – he thinks I'm his mate or something. He talks to me about this girl

158

who lives up the road – how pretty she is, how she'll never look twice at him… He's talking about my grandma and he's talking about her the way Nate talks to me about his girlfriend. Awkward, right? But other times, he knows exactly who I am and who he is – and he knows that my grandma died years ago. He's both those people at the same time, and he flips between one and the other faster than you can blink. So sure, there's something going on up there. Just because I don't understand it, that doesn't mean it isn't there, does it?"

"You really believe that?" She kept her eyes fixed on the lip of the coffee cup.

"Sure. Why not?"

A blast of guitar music came from Josh's pocket.

"Sorry. That's my phone – it'll be Nate. It's just a message. A couple of photos… Looks like he's having a ball at Hemisphere."

Someone shouting, "Nate! Over here!"

Blue.

Why is it always blue?

Blue. Naomi's favourite colour.

That stupid wig. The wig she bought when…

The wig.

"Josh…"

"Mmm?" He was still staring at his screen, flicking through pictures.

"Can … can I see those photos?"

"I guess…?" He gave her a quizzical look and handed her his phone.

They were pretty bad photos: some of them were blurry, half of them were dark. There were lots of shots of a group of guys waving their arms around, holding up cups of beer…

"Oh, wow," she said, swiping past what looked like someone climbing out of a tent, completely naked.

"Shit. Should've warned you about that one. Sorry…"

"Don't worry about it." She flicked some more – and before she knew it, she'd reached the last one.

The final picture was taken at night, in front of what looked like a circle of standing stones. The camera flash had been too close to whoever was in the photo – presumably Nate himself – and his face was a bright white blur.

But in the background…

Bex peered at the screen. She zoomed in on it, until it disintegrated into pixels.

Blue.

"Josh…"

"What?"

"Take this – don't move." She handed him back his phone and her hand was shaking so badly she almost dropped it.

"Bex? Are you OK?"

"Just … wait." She pulled out Naomi's laptop. "Wait. I want to…"

Blue.

She skimmed through Naomi's secret Facebook page, scrolling through photo after photo after photo. And there it was. She let out a triumphant "Ha!"

Wherever Naomi was in the photo, it was dark. She was wearing a white lace top that Bex had never seen. The wall behind her was covered with pages from comic books, illuminated by the bright flash of the camera.

But in this picture, Naomi's hair was blue. Bright blue, curling into a neat bob under her jawline.

"See that? She bought it a few months ago. I remember, because we had a massive fight afterwards." The memory of their disastrous shopping trip flashed through her mind – and the horrible argument that had come later, when Naomi had thrown the wig across the room. Bex had never thought about it again; not even when she'd seen that Facebook picture of her twin in a wig. She had simply forgotten it existed. But there it was. *Blue.*

"That's her in your photo. *That's my sister.*"

They stared at the phone.

"OK. OK, Bex. It could be anyone in that wig – you can't even see…"

"It's her. I *know* it's her." Bex took a deep breath.

161

"You know how there's always stories about twins? About how one knows the other one is in trouble?"

"You think Naomi's in trouble."

"Something happened. Something ... odd," she finished.

There was a long silence, and she waited for him to tell her she was crazy or to just walk out but he didn't. Instead, he was staring at her bookshelves. "Did you make this?" Josh was pointing to a small block of fired clay, pinched in places and twisted in others, sitting beside a stack of books. A neat hole ran all the way through it and in the middle was a tiny glass bead, suspended on fine gold wire. "You did! You made this. It's *amazing*. Is it part of your portfolio?"

"It's just something I made in free period at school. I wanted to try something..."

"You're not submitting it for your exams? How come?"

"I ... didn't want to?" The truth was, she didn't really know what to do with it. It didn't fit with anything she'd made for her exam: she hadn't done any sketches for it or written any notes – she'd just sat down with a lump of clay. "You really like it?"

"I do. It's very..." he shrugged, looking for the word, "you."

"You don't really know anything about me."

"Sure I do. I can see it all in there." He pointed to the

piece. "That's what art's for, isn't it? To explain something we can't put into words." He nodded at a postcard she'd taped to the wall: a Barbara Hepworth sculpture, one of her favourites. It was made up of two huge semicircles of bronze – a hole punched through each of them – fixed to a plinth so they looked like someone had cut clean through one whole circle with a knife. At first glance they appeared to be two halves of the same thing, but the more you looked at them, the more different and complete each half became. "'Two forms, divided circle', right?" Josh asked. "Have you been to the garden? Hepworth's, I mean."

"No. I want to, though."

"When you get up close to that one, something happens. It's like … you can see both the pieces and your brain's telling you that they should be two halves of a thing – but you can't make yourself believe it."

I have to tell him. I can't do this on my own.

"So, look. The twin thing," Bex began. "I have a… We have a…"

"You and your sister. Two forms, divided circle." He picked up the little sculpture and peered through it. "My grandad wakes up in the morning and he's seventy-five. He gets up, he gets dressed. And then all of a sudden, he walks out of the front door and he's lost fifty years, and he's twenty-five years old and waiting for my dead grandma in the park. Sooner or later, he goes back to being seventy-five, and he's old and his wife's dead, and he knows who we are again. I don't know. I can't tell you one way or the other which reality is more real for him – just like I can't tell you one way or the other whether you're somehow connected to your sister and she's connected to you." He paused and looked carefully at her. "Is that what happened in the coffee shop?"

"I don't know. I've never had them before…"

Except that's not true, is it? You'd just forgotten.

What about that first day of school? What about the time she got stuck in the cupboard at nursery and you sat down in the middle of the playground screaming that everything had gone dark? Falling out of the tree. Chickenpox.

"You don't think I'm crazy?"

"Let's say I'm open-minded."

"Even if I'm wearing ridiculous pyjamas?"

"*Especially* if you're wearing ridiculous pyjamas."

21

Naomi

Aged seven

"Will you two stop dawdling? We're late enough as it is!"

Naomi shakes her foot as she walks, trying to shift the stone that has caught between her foot and the inside of her trainer. She stops and Bex almost walks straight into her: she's too busy looking around at the Christmas lights. She tugs her trainer off her foot and turns it over: a tiny pebble bounces along the pavement.

"It felt *much* bigger than that."

"Rebecca! Naomi! Come on!"

The window of the hairdresser's is completely steamed up. Coloured shapes move behind the cloudy white: people in Christmas jumpers, putting on coats. As Naomi and Bex slip through the open door, the warm smell of the salon – hairspray and shampoo – wraps around Naomi like a scarf.

The hairdresser points them at the sofa by the window. Naomi rummages through the bowl of chocolates on the table and finds a single toffee among all the strawberry fondants. Bex is too wrapped up in the book full of hairstyles to be interested in anything else. Sometimes they look through the look-book together and Naomi makes up stories about every photo; who the people are and what their lives are like.

Not today, though. Today, she's left to stare at the cut-out snowflakes stuck on the front of the reception desk and count the twists in the paper streamers that criss-cross the ceiling.

"Who's first today?"

The hairdresser looks expectantly at Bex but she doesn't even glance up. There's a long pause … and then, "Looks like it's you, Naomi! Come on over."

Naomi settles into the chair and stares at herself in the mirror as the hairdresser combs out her hair. "Goodness, it's got long! What are we doing today, then? Just a trim?" She rests her hands on Naomi's shoulders … and suddenly she has the strongest feeling.

She looks at herself in the mirror and she can already picture herself running a hand through short hair, flicking it from side to side…

"I'd like it short, please." Naomi rests her hand against the side of her jaw. "To here?"

"Sure?"

When she gets up from the chair, Naomi turns to look over at the sofa, where Bex is looking at her with an expression of pure fury.

22

Naomi

Cold and nauseous, as Naomi stumbled back up the hill from the healer's tent she wondered whether she should try to get backstage again one last time – if she could find something to eat and somewhere warm to sit, she'd feel better.

But the thought of Ethan looking at her from behind the fence and then turning away... No doubt he'd gone back to the green room and laughed about it.

She hadn't pictured it like this. What had she been *thinking*?

The tent. The tea. All of it.

Naomi shivered, pulling the borrowed hoodie more tightly round her. Dew was starting to form on the bobbles of fleece. She must have been in the tent much longer than she had realized. How much time had she lost? She shook her head in disgust. To think she'd almost believed that psychic mumbo jumbo; believed there was some way she could cut away everything that wasn't Naomi. That she could just ... be free.

Might as well cut herself in two.

She'd thought she was protecting herself from pain. She'd thought it would be like closing a door and throwing away the key; a simple cut, an exorcism that rid her of something she no longer wanted ... but that wasn't it at all. What she had seen was dark and cold and lonely. Untethered. Lost and adrift.

If it had gone further, then she wouldn't just have lost Bex. She would have lost everything.

She had thought she wanted to be free from Bex ... but Bex wasn't the problem, was she? She never had been.

At the top of the hill, the group in the middle of the stone circle had lit a campfire and were huddled round it, draped in blankets.

Between the star-speckled darkness above and the festival lights shining below, Naomi felt like she was weightless.

She needed to get home. The thought rang through her as clear as a bell.

Maybe we can still fix it. Maybe we can.

It had come so close to being unfixable. It could have been ... but it wasn't. And now Naomi could see what she had almost done, her skin crawled.

I almost lost her. For real, forever.

I don't want to lose her.

I can't.

I have to get home.

Naomi counted off her options on her fingers: Find the band (somehow) and convince them (somehow) to give her a ride home. Unlikely.

The security office. She could report her stolen bag and use the phone to call home.

Maybe her dad would come and get her...

But she didn't want to be rescued. Bad enough that there would be trouble for going to Hemisphere in the first place; there was no need to make it any more humiliating by giving them the chance to treat her like a child, coming to collect her and lecturing her all the way back.

No. She would have to find her own way home ... which meant waiting until morning and hitching.

"Hello there?" One of the group by the campfire had turned to look at her. "Do you want to sit by the fire for a minute? You look a little cold..." The girl shuffled to one side to make space.

"I lost my friends." She had to say something and it was meant to be casual but it came out pathetic and small. "We were supposed to be meeting..."

"Oh, I'm sure they'll find you soon enough. You can wait here if you like?"

The fire was so welcoming. She could sit, couldn't she? Just for a minute...

"No, thanks. I'd better go look for them – they'll never

find me up here. Thanks, though." She smiled.

"Good luck!" The girl turned away, wrapping herself more tightly in the blanket draped around her shoulders.

Looking down at the site made Naomi feel even smaller. To one side, the main stage – now closed for the night – loomed over the arena field. Most of the food stalls were dark, too, and the handful still lit had long queues snaking away from the counters. The smell of frying onions wafted through the air, making her stomach growl … then churn. She trudged down the hill towards the stage. The walkway that cut through to the backstage area was closed off; another section of wire fencing dragged across it and padlocked in place.

So that was that – even if she had wanted to try and find Ethan and the others, she had no choice but to keep going through the night. It would be OK. She just needed to keep moving, find something to do. It was a festival, after all – something would be happening somewhere, so she might as well enjoy it … and deal with tomorrow tomorrow.

On the far side of the food stalls was what looked like a small, brightly lit village. As she got closer, she could see what she hadn't noticed earlier: it had high walls around it, covered in what looked like tinfoil. She'd assumed it was some kind of utility area or the back of a bank of toilets – but now, with two massive doors flung open and dry ice pouring out, it was unmissable. The place was swarming with people heading that way, following bass so loud that it made her ribs vibrate. The huge illuminated letters over the entrance read 'XANADU'.

Here was a place where *everyone* would be up all night.

The lights got closer, brighter, and the sound of people rose to a steady hum. A couple of stilt-walkers stalked past and a guy dressed in a bright red morphsuit crowd-surfed. Another morphsuit passed, this time black, lit up with hundreds of white LEDs. Ahead, there was a stage where dancers in costumes made from blue and purple ribbons whirled alongside a DJ and an acrobat spun high overhead, suspended from a crane.

"Coming through! Mind your backs – careful, sir, wouldn't want you to lose any of that fine beard you've got there!"

Naomi turned to see where the voice was coming from and spotted a juggler moving through the crowd, grinning as he tossed knives in the air.

"Easy, easy… I'm a professional, you know," the juggler said as he passed, shooting Naomi a broad smile. "Great hair, gorgeous!"

The crowd closed around him.

Naomi…

It was barely more than a whisper but she heard it.

"I know," she said, and the relief made her want to

shout. But almost as fast as she felt it, it darkened and something twisted underneath her heart – because Bex had waited until now, until it had come to this, to reach for her. Naomi shivered and turned away.

Beside her, a group of five or six people were passing round a small plastic bag. Naomi saw one of them slip something under his tongue as he turned away from the centre. Seeing Naomi watching him, he gave her a knowing smile. As soon as he did, Naomi recognized the floppy hair, the white shirt, the pendant…

"Hello again."

"Max!" Naomi beamed at him out of sheer relief at seeing someone she recognized.

"Told you I'd see you around, didn't I? And I see this came in handy?" He tugged playfully at the sleeve of the hoodie.

"Thanks. It's been a lifesaver."

Max held out his closed fist to her. "Trick or treat." He waited for her to open her hand, then held his over it and unclenched his fingers.

A pill dropped into her palm. There was a tiny smiley face stamped on the top of it.

Why not?

She had made such a mess of everything and she was tired and she was angry. Angry at herself for being here, for letting things come to this. Angry at her parents.

Angry at Bex for being so perfect; for being a reflection she could never match.

But tomorrow was tomorrow and Max was still there, smiling and holding out his hand – his fingers outstretched.

23

Bex

Aged five

The school isn't what Bex was expecting. She thought it would be one classroom – the blue one they saw before, with the bright yellow sun painted on the wall. She thought they would all be together.

She stands in the doorway, looking at all the other children. Some of them have already picked up crayons, some of them know each other, too.

Bex doesn't know anyone. That's not true.

Bex knows Naomi. But Naomi isn't there.

The teachers say it will be better if they're in separate classes, make it easier for them to settle in and make friends. She feels a familiar, anxious tug deep inside her.

"Bex? Where's your classroom? Is it next to mine?"

"I think so. I don't know. Do you think they're going to keep us apart all the time? I don't want to be apart."

"Me neither. My classroom's blue. What about yours?"

"Green."

"That's not so bad. You like green!"

Bex isn't convinced but the teacher smiles at her and

beckons her over. She says something but all Bex can hear is Naomi babbling away in her head.

"I have to go. I'll find you at playtime, I promise."

Bex steps hesitantly into her new classroom.

24

Naomi

As daylight crept across the festival site, everything was slowly bleached a gloomy shade of grey. The lights became a little less dazzling, the dancers a little less energetic and a trampled, muddy field speckled with empty plastic cups. As Xanadu gradually shut down, the crowds turned and stumbled up the hill towards the camping fields.

The clouds had gathered through the night and the sky was heavy with rain but Naomi didn't care.

New dawn, new day, new Naomi.

Of course, she still had the small problem of home to deal with – getting there, for a start, and then her parents, who would probably ground her until she was forty. And then there would be Bex. How could she make things better between them? Where would she even start?

She stopped at the top of the hill and looked back over the site. Suddenly, it seemed so different. So small. The slope flattened out into a collection of lumpy fields. To the left, a path made from plastic matting led to the camping fields. To the right, another path headed to the funfair.

The two of them, Naomi and Bex, standing in front of the waltzers. One of them had insisted on going on. The other hadn't wanted to and had cried the whole time.

She couldn't remember which had been her. The more she thought about it, the more clearly she remembered first one side of the memory and then the other.

She stared at the gondolas of the little ferris wheel, rocking gently in the breeze. In front of her was a plastic sign pointing to various camping areas, toilets, the security office and a car park and exit.

She could find her own way home, on her own terms.

Just like she could fix things with Bex, on her own terms.

Stifling a yawn, she picked her way past the funfair towards the exit. There were a couple of staff opening the hook-a-duck stall, and just for a moment, Naomi was sure she saw something flicker at the corner of her eye; smelled coffee in the air as clearly as if she were holding it in her own hand.

Bex's cat pyjamas.

Coffee.

Pyjamas.

Checked shirt.

Cake crumbs.

Freckles.

The breeze was stronger up on the top of the hill than it was down in Xanadu – but even though it whipped blue strands from her wig into her face, it made her feel alive. Maybe it was time to leave the wig behind, too. Make it … symbolic.

A guy wearing a bright yellow steward's jacket was leaning against the gatepost through to an overflow car park. He didn't notice Naomi until she stood right in front of him.

"Hi!" she said brightly. "Do you know where I can get a lift to town?"

"To town? Now?" He raised an eyebrow at her.

"Hey, I've been looking for you!" The shout came from behind her, and she whipped round to see Max walking towards her.

In the unforgiving morning light, he looked older than she'd thought he was. He was in his twenties, and the skin around one of his eyes looked shiny … like the beginning of a black eye. His white shirt was still pristine, and somehow his shoes didn't even have a speck of mud on them. He had his bag on his shoulder and scrapes on his knuckles, clearly visible as he held the strap with one hand. Following her gaze, he shifted his grip and held out the cup he was carrying.

"Coffee?"

"Thanks." She took a swig.

Max nodded. Considering he'd been up all night, too, his eyes were just a tiny bit too wide-awake. "Enjoy the party last night?"

"The party was good. The party was *necessary*."

"The party usually is." He grinned again.

"Thank you, by the way. For helping me out yesterday." She looked up at him from below her eyelashes. "My knight in shining armour."

"I try."

"Sir Max. Wanna help a damsel out?"

"How can I be of assistance, my lady?"

"I need a ride."

"Oh, do you?" His eyebrows twitched suggestively.

"To town." She smiled at his joke ... even though she didn't find it funny. But it was part of the game, wasn't it?

"Which one?"

"Whichever's closest."

"Well..." he shifted the bag on his shoulder, "in that case, today must be your lucky day. I was just heading out myself."

"That would be amazing – thank you!" She stopped and cleared her throat. "Sorry. I'm totally taking advantage of you, aren't I? You've been so nice."

"Think nothing of it."

There was something different about him compared to last night. Maybe he was tired. Naomi studied him again. Maybe she was supposed to have met him: maybe this was how it was meant to go, after all?

In no time at all, Naomi was settled into the passenger seat of Max's blue Mini and Hemisphere, Ethan … everything … was lost to the rear-view mirror. Naomi stared out of the window, watching the fields slide by on the other side of the glass. The car had a faintly unpleasant chemical smell about it. Despite the fact the morning air was cool, Max rolled down both their windows and put the air blower on its coldest, fastest setting.

"Fresh air. Blow the cobwebs away." He sniffed and swivelled his head to look at her. "You look like you could use it," he said.

Naomi shrugged away the comment. "My hair's a mess from being under the wig. The price of beauty, right?"

He nodded, curling his fingers more tightly around the steering wheel. "If you want, you can have a shower at mine before I drop you in town. After last night, you could probably do with one, right?"

Naomi ignored the comment and the smirk that went with it. "You do this a lot, do you? Festivals, I mean?" she added, seeing his eyes slide from the windscreen to his bag in the back seat. He was constantly checking it: a hand reaching for it or resting on it, a quick glance every couple of minutes.

"Now and again." He pressed a button on his door and

both windows slid back up.

His voice dropped. "I owe a few people."

"Oh?" Naomi knew better than to ask but he seemed to want to talk, so she let him.

"It wasn't my fault. It was Ibiza."

"Ibiza? Like – the place?"

He twitched when she spoke – almost as though he'd forgotten she was there.

"I was out there a couple of years ago. Ran up some debts, and there was this…" He stopped again, abruptly. "A man needed a hand, is all."

Another glance at the back seat.

She gave him a smile and slid down in her seat as the car chewed through the miles to the nearest town.

25

Bex

"You and your sister…"

"Naomi," Bex said.

"Naomi. Right." Josh smiled. "Let's say this twin-thing is real. How does it work?" He'd been sitting in the garden waiting for her to change out of her pyjamas.

"I don't know. I think I forgot, or she did, or … something," she finished. A bee buzzed past her, right in front of her nose, and she swatted it away. "It's tricky. The only thing I can think of is that it's like those doors you get between rooms in a hotel; the ones you can open to join the rooms together. Each one has a lock. If you don't open them both, you can't get through. Does that make sense?"

"Uh-huh…" said Josh – and she couldn't tell whether he meant it, or was just saying it to humour her.

"I think it was like that. And one of the doors got shut."

Was it mine? Was it hers?

Two teachers waiting for them in the office; understanding that they weren't going to be allowed to stay together. Being told it would be better this way.

"I think it was when we started primary school." Bex shut her eyes against the memory. "I'd almost forgotten. I thought it was just a game we used to play. But it can't have been. I remember things – things that I don't think actually happened to *me*. They happened to *Naomi*. It's like…" She waved her hands in exasperation. "Like the doors, right? Where does one room start and the other stop? No wonder she's so angry with me. She thinks I let her down. Worse, she thinks I did it on purpose. This is all my fault."

"It's not your fault, Bex." Josh shook his head. "You didn't know, did you?"

"I should have, though. That's the *point*."

Bex grabbed for the wall as the world twisted sideways … and she fell. Her head hit the paving – hard. There were lights dancing in front of her eyes. Red, yellow and bright white.

Someone holding out their hand … his hand.

Angry.

Flashing flashing flashing…

"Bex!" Hands on her shoulder. "Here – slowly. I've got you." Gently Josh eased her upright as the garden came back into focus. "How's your head? You banged it pretty hard."

Blue.

"Listen, Josh... Your friend Nate – the one who's at Hemisphere. Can you call and ask him if he knows anything about the girl with blue hair."

He looked at her skeptically. "And then what? What if he *has* seen her?"

"I don't know!"

"Fine. But if he yells at me for waking him up, you're dealing with him."

He pulled out his phone and dialled, not taking his eyes off her for a second.

"Yeah? No. No, mate. Sorry. I need a favour..." Another pause. "There's a girl." Another pause, this time with an eye-roll. "Funny, yeah. She's a friend's sister... *No*. She's done a bunk and they're trying to find her." Another pause. "She's in one of the photos you sent me. Yeah. I know. Last night... Yeah, all right, I know. But they're really worried, OK? And it's me asking."

Another pause. "Blue wig. Brown eyes...?" His expression shifted into something unreadable and Bex's heart sped up.

"You did? Where? Last night. You're sure? Yeah, yeah. *With* somebody? Who?" Josh frowned, glanced at Bex and looked away again, quickly. "And she... Mmm. OK. No, no worries. Yeah. Yeah, soon. All right."

He hung up, and looked hesitantly back at Bex. "Slightly unbelievably, he actually did see her. Last night."

"He did?"

"In Xanadu – it's the after-hours part of the site. Clubbing, dancers, all that. She was with this guy…"

"Right…?"

"A dealer."

26

Naomi

With the windows closed, the smell of the car was starting to give Naomi a headache. She pushed the button to lower hers but nothing happened.

"Child locks," said Max, not taking his eyes off the road.

"You have kids?" she said automatically.

He didn't answer.

Max wasn't looking too well. A thin film of sweat coated his forehead. Even as she watched him, he leaned forward and flicked the heater on, turning it up as high as it would go. Then he turned it off. Then he turned it on again. The further they got from the festival site, the twitchier he seemed to become; he kept sniffing and rubbing his nose. Every now and again he glanced at himself in the rear-view mirror, stretching his neck and peering at his eyes.

It was fine. She wasn't feeling especially great, either. She was tired, and she was fairly sure she smelled. She'd thank him for the lift, take him up on the offer of using his bathroom to wash her face and freshen up, and then she'd go.

Home.

Max checked his eyes in the mirror again. Naomi told herself to ignore it.

After another few turns and a couple of roundabouts, he finally pulled the car in to the side of a residential street. It looked the same as every other street they'd driven down for the last ten minutes and it occurred to Naomi that she had no idea where she was.

And nor, whispered a quiet voice inside her head, did anyone else.

Max switched off the engine. "Home, sweet home." They were outside a scruffy-looking terrace with rubbish dumped in the tiny paved front yards of every house. The one they were parked outside had a metal security grille over the front door and grubby curtains pulled tightly closed across all the windows. Beneath the metal, the blue paint was peeling off the door.

"Not exactly Camelot, but it's always good to come home after a festival – right?" He slipped out of the driver's seat, slamming the door behind him and darting round to open her door. "My lady."

He opened the boot of his car and peered into it. "Where's your stuff?" he asked, pointing at the empty boot.

"My stuff? I … didn't have any – remember?"

"You went to a festival with no stuff?"

"My bag got stolen. That was how we met. You gave me your hoodie?" She tugged at the sleeve.

"I've never seen that before in my life," he muttered. He went to slam the boot shut but his hand missed it, swinging down through the empty air … and seeing him twist, off-balance, she reached out a hand to stop him before he fell.

His free hand snapped out, locking shut around the back of her neck. Tightly.

His grip lasted maybe a second, perhaps two, but it felt longer. Every single point where his fingertips connected with her skin *hurt*. As unexpectedly as he had grabbed her, he let go – giving her a sheepish smile.

"Sorry about that. Thought I was going over." He closed the boot of the car, peering through the window to check his bag on the back seat. "Thanks."

She could smell the chemicals on his breath and in his sweat.

"I think…" he muttered. He checked the street – once, twice. There wasn't anyone around and Naomi wasn't sure what he was looking for, but it wasn't there. He draped an arm round her shoulder, and even though it felt casual and friendly, a little alarm bell rang even more insistently.

"You know, Max… I should head off pretty soon. I might give that shower a miss."

"What?" He fumbled with the lock on the door. "I insist." Finally getting the door itself open, he half fell through it – dragging Naomi with him. "Straight up to the first floor," he said.

When the door slammed back into place, Naomi felt it all the way through her body. All she had to do was get him up to his flat, settle him down … and leave.

His flat – more of a bedsit than a flat, really – could have been nice if it hadn't been so chaotic… Or if he hadn't locked the door behind them, pulling out the key. He tugged open the greying curtains and kicked off his shoes. There wasn't much furniture: a double bed tucked in the far corner and a small cooker across from it, a couple of narrow shelves beside that holding plates and cups, a table and two chairs – one with a broken back – and then a door into what must be the bathroom. None of it went with the way he was dressed, the way his hair was cut. It felt like somebody else's home…

He tucked the door key on the shelf with the plates. "Can't be too careful."

She thought back to the rucksack he'd left in the car, in plain view on the back seat. "You're not worried about your bag?"

"My ba…? Oh. No. No, no." He sniffed loudly and rubbed the end of his nose so hard with his hand that it flattened against his palm. "Not mine, anyway. Tea. Tea,

tea, tea," he mumbled, picking up a flimsy kettle and waving it at her. "How d'you take it?"

"You know," she said as casually as she could, "I'll take a raincheck on the tea. I had no idea it had got so late in the…"

"How d'you know the time? You're not wearing a watch." He shoved the kettle under the tap and filled it.

"Oh. The clock." She nodded to the clock hanging on the wall across the room.

"I wouldn't pay any attention to that. It's been wrong for years. A cup of tea's the least I can do before you go."

"It's really sweet of you. But I've just remembered I promised I'd call my boyfriend…"

"What's his name? Your boyfriend?"

His back was to her as he reached for two mugs from the shelf. She couldn't see his face but something in his tone had changed.

"Josh." She picked the first name that came to mind.

"How come he wasn't at Hemisphere with you?"

"Oh, he isn't really into festivals. Not his thing, you know?"

"And he doesn't get jealous?"

"Jealous? No! He's not like that." She laughed. And then she did the one thing Dan had told her she should never, ever do. She added more to the lie. "And he's got flu. So even if he did want to come…"

"And you're running back to look after him, are you? How ... sweet." The kettle clicked off. "I don't think you're telling me the whole truth, are you?" He lifted the kettle and poured water in both the mugs. His hand was shaking and he'd forgotten to put the tea bags in.

She took a step back as he moved towards the table, sliding the mugs across the top. Water sloshed out of them both but he didn't notice, pulling up a chair and easing himself into it, yanking his phone out from his pocket and dropping it on the table in front of him. He kicked the other chair out from under the table with his toe.

"Sit."

"I'm OK over…"

"I said SIT."

She sat.

"I've been wondering about you."

"Is that so?" She reached for the nearest mug.

"Bit of a coincidence, wasn't it, you being at the exit I happened to be leaving by – and needing a lift? Especially after we kept bumping into each other like that."

"Small world, right?" She shrugged, lifting the mug to her lips with a smile.

"No wallet, no phone…"

"You know they were stolen. You were there."

"Nothing to prove you are who you say you are," he said. "I mean, you could be anyone, couldn't you?"

He swallowed a mouthful of scalding water, apparently not noticing that it wasn't tea – nor how hot it was.

"I really should get going…" If she said it enough times, maybe he would hear it…

He didn't move.

"Here's an idea!" She leaned forwards and brazenly picked up his phone, ignoring the way his whole body tensed. "Let me put my number in your contacts, and when I get a new one, I can call you? We could meet up, go for a drink?"

Her fingers flew across the keypad – his phone wasn't locked, which struck her as odd, but it was lucky for her. She had tapped in a made-up number and her first name before he even registered what she was saying. Trying not to let her hand shake, she twisted the phone as much as she dared and opened the camera…

"What are you doing?" His speech was slower than before; as though he had just woken up or was looking up at her from the bottom of an ocean.

"Putting my number in, like I said – nearly done…"

She opened up the messaging app, typed in Bex's number – for a heart-stopping moment, she wasn't sure she could remember it – and flicked back to the camera.

"Put the phone down."

"One sec…"

There was no time. She hit the shutter button, attached

the photo and pressed 'send' without even looking at what she'd taken – closing everything an instant before he leaned forward and snatched the phone with one hand.

His other hand slammed down on to her knee, under the table. She flinched and tried to pull away – but his grip was like iron.

She watched him scroll through his contacts, stopping when he reached her number.

"Nay-oh-mee."

She gave him a smile.

But then he narrowed his eyes. "Did you just send somebody a message on my phone, Nay-oh-mee?"

He placed the phone flat on the table, jabbed at it a few times and sat back. The sound of dialling squeaked out of the speaker.

Don't answer it. Don't answer it. Don't answer it.

Naomi thought it harder than she had ever thought anything in her life.

I'm waiting. Waiting. Don't leave me here. Don't…

Find me. Find me like I always found you.

"Hi, this is Bex. Sorry I can't answer right now – but if you leave me a message I'll call you right back…"

Max's face was a picture of rage as he poked another finger at his phone and the line went dead. "Who. Is. Bex?"

27

Bex

The woman at the other end of the Hemisphere office phone line was less than helpful. "Look, I'm very sorry – but it's really nothing to do with us. Even if she is here, I don't know what we're supposed to do about it."

"But you…"

"If it's a police matter, the police should get in touch with our security team directly and we will – of course – do everything we can to help. In the meantime…"

"In the meantime, you won't help me?"

"Look, Rebecca – it was Rebecca, wasn't it?"

"Yes. Rebecca Harper. My sister's name is Naomi."

"Yes. I'm afraid there's nothing I can do right now. If your sister's here, accompanied by someone over the age of eighteen, then she's not breaking any of our regulations."

"And if she isn't?"

"Then I'm afraid you'd have to prove that. And you're telling me she's here on a band's guest pass – is that right?"

"Yes."

"Can you tell me the name of the band?" There was an

expectant pause.

"I don't know."

"Right. So you can't tell me who she's with."

"No."

"And you're absolutely sure she's here, are you?"

"Yes!"

The conversation was just going to go round and round. Bex hung up and stomped back out into the garden, where Josh was fiddling with his phone. He looked up as she dropped on to the bench next to him.

"No joy?"

She shook her head.

"Nate just messaged me – he bumped into a guy at the bar…"

"And?"

"He was wearing a bright blue wig."

"Naomi's wig? Where did he get it? Was she there?"

"She wasn't there but Nate asked him about it, and this guy turns out to be one of the locals who's helping with the stewarding. He says he saw a girl, who gave him the wig, leaving the site this morning with a guy."

"The same guy?"

"From what Nate can figure out, yes. It sounds like the same guy."

"So now she's left the site and we don't know where she's gone."

They both stared at the paving in front of them.

Absently, she rubbed at a spot on the back of her neck. It felt like someone had poked her…

"Ow," she muttered, rubbing again … and just as suddenly as it had started to hurt, it stopped. Josh was looking at her again. "Don't ask," she said.

"I think you should go to the police. She could be in serious trouble."

Bex's phone chirped. Someone had sent her a message. "It's probably just Kay again…"

But the number was withheld … and there was no text. Just a photo.

Josh leaned in, peering at it with her.

"What … is that?"

"I'm not sure. A clock?"

The photo was blurry, as though it had been taken by accident.

It was a wall, part of the ceiling above it and a slightly grubby white plastic clock – which, if the photo had just been taken, was an hour and a bit slow.

"Why would someone send you a picture of a clock?" Josh asked.

Bex shook her head. "Maybe it was an accident."

"Mmm. Can I?" Josh held out his hand and Bex passed him the phone, watching as he turned it round and round.

"Wait!" she cried. "Look. There. In the corner."

"That's ... that's an ear, isn't it?" Josh squinted at the pinkish blur.

"Whoever took that photo, they're not on their own. And they have my number."

The phone started to ring.

Still huddled over it, Bex and Josh stared.

"It's the same person, isn't it?" Josh whispered.

"Don't answer it. Don't answer it. Don't answer it."

Naomi's voice was clear.

"Find me. Find me like I always found you."

"You're not going to answer it?"

"I…"

The phone stopped ringing. Josh was staring at her like she was *actually* insane. But Bex had never felt more sure. Naomi had sent her the photo, she *knew* it. She'd sent the photo – secretly, perhaps, in a hurry – but she'd been caught out. Bex had *heard* her, heard her sister in her head telling her not to answer the phone.

She rubbed the back of her neck again and stopped. Her fingers were resting exactly on the painful spots.

It had been a hand. A hand on Naomi's neck.

The clock.

Naomi.

"Find me."

If she could picture the clock…

She closed her eyes. There it was, just like it had been

197

in the photo – but less blurry. She could see it so clearly –
the wall around it. The ceiling above.

A small, dirty cooker. A kettle.

A chair with a broken back.

A key on a shelf.

A security gate.

A man, his back to her.

White shirt, khaki trousers.

And then it was all gone.

"I'll find you. I promise."

"Josh? I have an idea, and I need you to trust me."

As they walked up the ramp to the police station door,
Bex felt Josh's hand brush against hers.

It was quiet inside and it still smelled of bleach. Josh
nodded at the chairs in the waiting area. "D'you want to
sit down? I'll ask if Dionne's around…"

"No," said Bex. "I'll go." She walked over to the
reception desk where, behind the glass, a police officer
was sorting a pile of paperwork.

"Hi," she said. He stopped shuffling his papers and
looked at her. "Is Dionne around? I'm Rebecca Harper.
It's about my sister, Naomi. She's missing. Dionne said…"

"I'll call her for you. Take a seat." He picked up the handset
of a large grey desk phone and dialled an extension.

A clicking sound made her look at a chair behind her. The lady with the big hair and the knitting was still there. She was still knitting.

Bex gave her a smile. "Hello again," she said.

Knitting Lady raised an eyebrow at her.

Josh was fidgeting. She glanced up and down the hallway, trying to line up her thoughts into something that would make sense to a police officer with a notebook.

"It might take a while," Josh said.

"Then I'm just going to go…" She pointed down the corridor to the toilets.

In the bathroom, Bex splashed water on her face, patting her skin dry again with a paper towel. She blinked at her reflection in the mirror. Pink-rimmed and bloodshot eyes with dark circles beneath them blinked back at her … and when the mirror shimmered in front of her, there wasn't even time to think about what was coming. Ringing filled her ears, building and building to a scream. She pressed her hands to the side of her head knowing, even as she did it, that it wouldn't make any difference.

The room was spinning, faster and faster. Something jolted her forwards.

Clinging to the sink, she looked over her shoulder. The door was still closed. There was no one in there with her … and yet she had definitely felt a shove. Another one – and a hard, strong pinch on her arm.

"Bex!" Naomi was calling her.

"Naomi…"

There was another jolt, another blow, and this time, her feet were swept out from under her.

Bex…

Bex heaved herself up from the tiled floor. Her cheek throbbed and when she rubbed it, the skin felt tender under her fingertips. She stood up and looked in the mirror and there on her skin, right where it hurt, was the clear outline of a hand, as though someone had slapped her. And, as she stared at her reflection, she realized that the terrified brown eyes looking back out at her weren't her own. They were her sister's.

"Naomi!"

"Bex."

Bex pressed her fingers against the glass and the Naomi in the mirror did the same. Their fingertips touched and Bex could almost feel the warmth of her twin's skin…

And then it was just her own reflection looking back at her. She turned her head, checking her cheek … but there was nothing. Not even a hint of a mark.

She pulled herself together and shouldered her way back through the bathroom door.

"I'll find you, I promise."

After a little while, footsteps echoed down the corridor. "Rebecca," said a calm voice. "I'm Dionne Ambrose, the family support officer." She seemed sterner than Bex had hoped she would. "Hello, Joshua – I didn't know you two knew each other. How's your grandfather today?"

"Better, thanks," he said, sitting up. "Dad says he left his coat here?"

"I'll ask the duty officer. They've probably put it in the cupboard. Rebecca, shall we go somewhere we can talk?" She gestured to an interview room.

"Thanks. Can Josh come, too?"

Dionne raised an eyebrow. "We're only having a chat, so I don't think that should be a problem."

As they followed her, Josh whispered, "You OK?"

"Fine," she whispered back as Dionne waved them through an open door and gestured for them to take a seat on one side of the little table.

"So, what was it you wanted to talk about? You said someone has seen Naomi?"

"She was at Hemisphere. The festival. One of Josh's friends saw her."

"Josh?" Dionne glanced up from the notes she was making.

He nodded and mumbled something about how it had been a nightmare for Nate to get a ticket because the website kept crashing and people online started saying that it was sold out but then…

"Yes, I've heard it's hard to get tickets," Dionne interrupted. "They sell out months before, don't they?"

"She was given a guest pass," Bex cut in, shooting Josh a look of disbelief.

"A guest pass?" Dionne made a note in her book. "By whom?"

"I ... don't know?"

"You don't know."

Josh came to the rescue. "Nate said he saw her."

"And he's sure it was her?"

"We've got a photo." He pulled out his phone, flipping through the images until he found the one with Naomi in the background.

Dionne frowned. "It's not very clear, is it? You're sure?"

"I'm sure," said Bex. "We think she's with someone."

"The person who gave her a guest pass?"

"No – it wasn't..." Everything up to this point had been true, more or less. But beyond this, it got complicated.

She gave a quick sideways glance at Josh. His gaze locked on to hers and held it.

"Rebecca?"

Finally Bex managed to force the words out of her mouth. "Nate – Josh's friend – said the guy she's with ... might be a dealer."

28

Naomi

"I said: who … is … Bex?"

"She's … she's my sister, OK?"

"And why are you sending her photos of my flat?"

"I wasn't!"

He held up his phone, screen out. There was the photo. She felt the blood drain from her face. She hadn't managed to get him in the picture. What good was a photo of a clock going to be?

"You weren't, were you?"

He tossed the phone aside – it slipped from the table and landed somewhere on the floor. He picked up the mug again as though he was going to drink from it…

Then he smashed it on the tabletop, tiny ceramic shards flying up and hot water splashing her face. "Who are you?" He was still holding the handle of the mug in his hand. "Did Toby send you?"

"Who's Toby?"

"Because you can tell him – I *have* the money. I'm almost there."

"I don't know what you're talking about…" She tried to pull away but it was no use.

"It's here. You tell him!" He waved his hand – still clutching the shattered mug handle – wildly at the room, and then he was on his feet and pacing back and forth. "Or maybe you're not here for Toby… Why are you here?" He didn't give her any time to answer, just kept talking faster and faster. "Someone like you, just waiting. Needing to be rescued. You knew I would, didn't you? You were counting on it."

"What? I don't…"

"You're one of *them*, aren't you?" He moved to the window and, pressing himself up against the wall beside it, peered out at the street. "I knew it."

"I'm not anyone. I just had my stuff stolen and you helped. And then you were leaving and you offered me a lift. That's it. End of story." She kept her voice level, even though inside she was screaming. Could she get the key? Could she get out before…

"Right." His shoulders relaxed and his breathing slowed. "But you owe me. My bag still had some gear in it and that's gone now."

"Your bag? Your bag's in the car. You left it in the back."

"No, I didn't."

"You did. Look out of the window – I bet you can see it from up here."

"You had it."

"I didn't! I swear to you, if you look out of the window…"

But he wasn't listening. "I'll have to explain that to Toby. Maybe you should come with me…"

"I thought you said you had his money."

"I thought you said you didn't know who Toby was," he said, his full attention suddenly on her.

"I don't – I… I'm going to go now," she said.

"No – wait. Wait." He stopped. "I'm sorry. You lost your phone. You wanted to let your…" he paused, "*sister* know where you were. I overreacted. Call her. Use the landline, if you like." He smiled at her but it didn't reach his eyes. "It's right there by the door."

She felt him watching her as her eyes flicked over to a battered handset and on to the door. All she wanted to do was get out.

"Well, go on then. Call her. Or maybe you'd rather call your boyfriend." His voice was like the flat of a knife blade.

"Yes. My boyfriend."

"The one who's sick with the flu? He won't mind that you're here. After all, he was fine with you going off to a festival all by yourself, wasn't he?"

"What? Why would…?"

The room was getting smaller, darker.

"I'll find you. I promise."

He was across the room to her again, so quickly. He was so close that she could feel his breath on her ear. His fingers tightened around her hair and it hurt. Her scalp burned as he twisted her head towards him…

His hand connected with her cheek, sending her spinning to the floor.

He was talking as he stood over her – she could see his lips moving, but she couldn't hear it over the noise in her ears. She shook her head to clear it, slowly pulling herself to her feet.

A noise from out on the street caught his attention – he turned his head towards the window and Naomi saw her chance. She kicked out at him as hard as she could. Her foot connected with his ankle and he yelped in surprise and pain, and crashed to the floor, grabbing for her as he fell. But she was too quick and she leaped out of reach. She snatched up the second mug of still-hot water on the table, throwing it right at him. He shrieked in shock as the water splashed his face … and Naomi hurled herself into the bathroom, praying the door had a lock.

She slammed it closed, turned the lock with relief and leaned back against the wood. He threw his weight against it, trying to force it even though the door opened outwards. The whole door trembled as he banged his fist on it over and over and over again. Finally, he stopped and she could hear him swearing and limping across the floor.

She tugged on the light pull and somewhere above her an extractor fan rattled into life along with the bulb. No window. There was a bath with a dirty soap-scum ring around it and a flimsy blue shower curtain. A sink and toilet, a mirrored cabinet on the wall.

A pair of nail scissors were balanced on the back of the sink behind the taps. They looked reasonably sharp – better than nothing, anyway.

Maybe if she waited long enough, he would pass out... She couldn't see any other way out. Maybe he'd go to get his bag, and she could run to the window and scream for help?

Her cheek throbbed.

Naomi leaned forward to check the damage in the mirror. It could have been worse, she supposed, closing her eyes and resting her forehead against the cool glass.

"I'll find you. I promise."

Naomi opened her eyes, tipping her face away from the mirror ... and froze.

It wasn't her face in the glass. It was Bex's.

29

Bex

Dionne studied the photo of the clock. "What am I looking at?"

"I … we … we think Naomi sent it. We think she's in trouble and she was trying to let us know where she is – or who she's with."

"She took the photo and sent it to you from her phone?"

"It's not her number. It's blocked. Isn't there something you can do to trace the number?"

Dionne sighed. "Not without a reason, Rebecca. And what…"

"And what if it is from Naomi? She's in trouble, I know she is!" Bex ran out of words and everything swam before her eyes.

"OK. OK. Let's take a step back." Dionne consulted her notes again. "This friend she was seen with…"

"He's not her friend," Bex interrupted.

"Do you know his name?"

"Well … no."

"Right. Then how are we supposed to do anything

about it?" She straightened her notebook in front of her, lining it up with the edge of the table, and rested her hands on the cover. "You can't give me a name, because you don't know."

"What if I recognized him?" Bex blurted out.

Dionne pursed her lips and Bex knew there was a chance where there hadn't been one before. She sat still, barely daring to breathe, and then finally, after an agonizing minute: "Let me make a phone call. No promises." Dionne closed the door behind her.

When she stepped back into the room, Josh was sitting with his head resting on his arms and Bex was staring up at the ceiling.

"You'd better come through."

The room she led them to this time was a little larger than the interview room. It had a desk with a couple of chairs and a large computer that looked like it was older than Bex.

"I'm giving you access to our secure photofit database."

"You're going to let us look through the photos?"

"You said she's with someone who was dealing drugs. If we know who he is, he'll be in here." Dionne tapped the computer. "Well, there you go. I've entered the most likely search parameters for you – take a look."

The screen had filled with tiny thumbnails.

Josh peered at them. "There's hundreds..." he groaned.

"Thousands, actually," Dionne added – then pointed to

a tiny black camera in the upper corner of the room. "I'll be keeping an eye on you…"

"This is hopeless."

Bex clicked through another row of pictures. None of the photos on the screen had looked the slightest bit familiar so far. She'd been hoping for something – a twinge of recognition. But there was nothing.

She had convinced Josh and Dionne – whose job it was not to be easily convinced – that she could do this. She had even convinced herself.

Why did I believe I could?

The answers were in her head. She had to believe it was real. She had to believe in Bex-and-Naomi.

She clicked on to the next page as Josh reappeared, carrying another cardboard tray of coffee cups.

"Here," he said, passing one to her.

She took it, barely looking up. "You drink a lot of coffee."

"I do. It's where I get my charm from."

"And there was me thinking it was all natural." She glanced over at him. "I don't even know what I'm looking for. I'm just … looking." She pointed to one at random. "This guy? Nope." She clicked again. "This one? Nope." And again. "Him? Nothing." One more time. "And this dude? Never seen him before in my life."

"Keep your voice down, Bex. Dionne's doing us a favour."

"It was a stupid idea. I'm so stupid. Stupid, stupid, stu…" The words gummed up her mouth.

It was him. She knew it was him.

Bex lurched forwards, grabbed the bin from under the desk and threw up.

She was vaguely aware of Josh disappearing through the door and then coming back with a cup of water. And Dionne.

Josh handed her the cup. "Bex?"

She pointed at the photo on the screen.

A bathroom. Small, dingy. Pounding on the door; the lock jolting further and further each time. Blue. Blue tiles. Blue tiles. A blue car. Blue wig. Blue. Blue. A backpack, a silver pendant. Smoke and a bitter, bitter taste. Blue. Cold. Chemicals. Wood. A blue door. Flickering torches. Smoke and chemicals and ceramic shards and flashing lights. Blue. Blue. Flashing lights.

It's all blue.

The images came faster and brighter. And behind them all, the ringing in her ears built until it drowned out everything else. She knew someone was talking to her but she couldn't make out anything but a drone. The only thing she could be sure of was the voice in her head.

"Bex."

She gulped the nausea back down. There was nothing left to throw up, anyway.

"She's been getting panic attacks since Naomi left." Josh was talking to Dionne. She could hear him as though he was far away or she was underwater. The world was swimming.

Dionne nodded and dropped into a crouch, her face level with Bex's.

"Rebecca, I need to be very clear. Do you recognize him?" She nodded. "You think Naomi might be with him?" She nodded. "I'll be right back."

Bex nodded again.

She wasn't sure how long Dionne was gone. When she came back, she was with a police officer.

"He's under a banning order for the next three years..." Dionne said. "Which means he's not permitted on any festival grounds. So if he's been at Hemisphere we can certainly pop over to his house for a talk."

"Has he?"

"We've got someone checking with the festival now. Anyone buying a standard ticket will have had to supply photo ID. He's almost certainly bought his ticket under a false name but he can't change his face."

Dionne's phone buzzed in her hand. "Yes?"

Bex held her breath.

"We've got him."

30

Naomi

Aged four

The slide is much, much higher than it looked from the bottom of the steps. Much higher.

Naomi stands at the top and looks down at the water rushing away beneath her feet. She wiggles her toes over the edge.

The others have gone down already. From her spot on the platform she can hear them, splashing and laughing.

But she's all alone at the top of the slide.

"*You're not all alone. I'm here,*" says Bex. "*Nothing bad can happen.*"

"It's so high."

"*It's not that high. It's just a water slide. Come on! Jump!*"

"I don't want to. I don't like it."

"*It's fun. Really. I promise.*"

"I'm not. I don't like it. It's too high! I want to come down…"

"*Then come down the slide.*"

"I don't want to."

"*Noom! Come on!*"

"Naomi? There you are!" Mrs Miller – Fern's mum – appears at the top of the slide steps, her hair wet from the swimming pool. "Is everything OK?"

"I... I got scared."

"Oh, sweetheart. That's OK – you don't have to go down the slide if you don't want to." Mrs Miller takes her hand and gives it a squeeze. "Let me help you down the steps."

"Yes, please." Naomi's so relieved she doesn't have to go down the slide that she feels sick.

"We're going to have another ten minutes in the pool and then we can get out and have something to eat. How does that sound?"

"OK."

Fern and Noah are climbing on the giant inflatable alligator that's floating in the water, Matthew and Harry are standing by their mum in the shallow part of the pool.

"Naomi?" Mrs Miller's voice is friendly. Naomi looks up at her: she's turning her head like she's trying to find someone else nearby. "Did I hear you talking to someone?"

Naomi smiles and nods. "I was talking to my sister."

"Your sister?" Mrs Miller looks over to where Bex is laughing and splashing a couple of the others. "Hasn't she been in the pool all this time?"

"Yes. She always talks to me in my head."

And she darts away to the pool and her twin, not noticing the strange look on Mrs Miller's face.

31

Naomi

He'd had another go at the door.

Thud. Thud. Thud.

Then the room on the other side of the door was quiet.

Naomi rested her head against the mirror – which reflected her face, and only hers. She had dark circles under her eyes and her lips were cracked.

She could wait, she thought. See if he fell asleep or passed out… But what if he already had and with every minute she let pass he was getting closer to waking up again?

Slowly, quietly, she reached for the lock on the door; holding her breath. It clicked as it turned.

Nothing. Nothing, nothing, nothing.

She edged the door open a crack. It was too still.

Too quiet.

His fingers clamped around the side of the door, tearing it away from her. She could see his knuckles turning white as she desperately fought to pull it back. Her grip on the handle was slipping – and sensing her hold loosening, he jammed his hand even further through the gap.

He was stronger than she was. If he let go, she could lock the door again. How could she get him to let go?

The scissors.

She twisted her body towards them, stretching one hand out. The tips of her fingers brushed the edge of the sink... Not close enough. She stretched further, further.

"Come on, come on..."

He yanked the door, swearing at her from the other side. It took all her strength and she wedged her feet on either side of the doorframe, bracing against the wood.

The scissors sat patiently on the sink.

Her spine screamed as she twisted and stretched as far as she possibly could. Her fingertip brushed metal and for one sickening moment she was afraid she had somehow pushed them even further out of reach. Then her fingertip hooked through the hooped handle – she had them.

In one single motion, she raised her arm and drove the scissors into the side of his hand.

He instantly released the door, yelling. She slammed it shut and locked it, still pulling against the handle with her heart racing.

Somewhere in the building there was a thumping sound, like someone knocking on a door. Had he called his friends?

There was a crash. Then thump-thump-thump-thump-

thump like someone running up the stairs. A knock on the door.

He was going to his front door, unlocking it. The front door squeaked as he opened it. His voice raised in surprise.

"Naomi? Naomi?"

She sat up straight. Someone was calling her name.

"Naomi Harper. Are you here? Naomi?"

"Here! I'm here!" She dragged herself to her feet and banged her palm against the door. "Hello? I'm here!"

"Naomi? Are you there? Are you hurt?"

"Who … who is it?" She could barely get the words out.

"This is the police, Naomi. You're safe. Open the door."

A prickle of fear ran down her spine.

There was silence on the other side – and then a new voice, a woman's. "We're here to take you home, Naomi."

"How do I know you are who you say you are?"

A rustling sound and then a small, laminated card slid under the door. An ID card.

"You can trust me, Naomi. Your sister Bex said to tell you that she found you."

Naomi opened the door.

The bedsit looked different with so many people in it: there were two uniformed police officers and the woman, dressed in a dark skirt suit. One of the officers was standing beside Max's bed – where he was sitting. He actually seemed a little pathetic, cradling his injured hand in one arm; he barely even glanced at Naomi as she stepped out of the bathroom.

The pose of the officer next to him was casual but his face was stern. The other, beside the front door, was speaking fast and low into a walkie-talkie, while the woman was obviously waiting for her to say something.

"I'm fine," she said, surprised at how calm she sounded. She didn't feel calm. "He didn't hurt me."

"Are you sure?"

"Yes. I'm OK. I am."

"There's a car waiting downstairs. We're taking you back to the station first – your parents and your sister are waiting for you there."

A small crowd had gathered around the police cars outside. Naomi ignored them as the woman ushered her towards the closest, a door already open for her, and she slid into the back seat.

There was already an officer in the driver's seat; the woman climbed into the empty passenger seat, took a phone from the driver and turned to face her.

"I've got your parents on the phone."

Naomi took the phone. It felt heavy. Everything felt heavy.

"*Get a grip,*" said a voice in her head.

She half grinned. Trust Bex to say that. She took the phone. "Hello?"

"Naomi!" Her mother's words were lost in sobs and then there was a scuffling sound, as though the phone was being handed over.

"Naomi?" Her father's voice. "Are you OK? What happened? Are you hurt…?"

"Dad. I'm fine. I'm so, so sorry."

"No, sweetheart. You don't have to be sorry. You're safe. You're coming home. That's all we want." There was a sniff on the other end of the line. "Bex is here. Do you want to speak to her?"

"No." Naomi shook her head. "I don't need to…"

"Noom! Don't say anything. This is you and me, remember? I'm sorry – I let other people get in the way. I let Kay get in the way. I didn't understand… But now I do. You and me. And that's how it's going to stay – I promise."

A wave of exhaustion threatened to engulf her, and it was all she could do to hand over the phone.

She was going home.

Bex

They were back in the interview room with Dionne again, but this time Bex's parents were squeezed in with them. Josh stood by the door, looking uncomfortable. Catching her eye, he gave her a half-smile and ducked out into the corridor. Stepping around her parents, she followed him.

"Josh! Wait! You're going?"

"This is a family thing. Besides," he held up his grandad's coat, "Dad sent me out for this *hours* ago."

"I couldn't have got through all this without you."

"I didn't do anything."

"Yeah, you did." She smiled at him. "I can't explain it…"

"Shocker," he muttered, but he was still grinning.

"I'm not sure I can ever thank you enough."

His smile lit up his whole face. "Sure you can. Next time – you get the cake."

"Next time?"

"Well, yeah. Obviously."

"Bex? She's here. The car's here."

Epilogue

Everything outside smells like rain: the tarmac, the air...
The white stripes on the black surface look like a bridge
leading to the police station door.

She takes a step along it. What will they say? How is she
going to explain everything?

And then a figure is running towards her. They collide,
the two of them, and cling to each other.

When they finally break apart, they stand face to face.
Two imperfect reflections: the same, but different. Naomi
sees Bex, and Bex sees Naomi. Each of them is totally
themselves and absolutely self-contained ... except for the
link that connects them.

Once it stood wide open, turning two minds into one.
But even when it's papered over and forgotten, a door is
still a door.

And a door can always be opened.

RED EYE

The
nightmare
begins
when you're
awake

SLEEPLESS

LOU MORGAN

About the Author

Lou Morgan is the award-nominated author of YA horror *Sleepless*, as well as two urban fantasy novels: *Blood and Feathers* and *Blood and Feathers: Rebellion*. She has been nominated for three British Fantasy Awards, twice for Best Fantasy Novel, as well as for the Hillingdon Secondary Book of the Year. She lives in Bath with her family and she tweets as @LouMorgan